Take the Mummy and Run

Read all the Carmen Sandiego™ Mysteries:

HASTA LA VISTA, BLARNEY

COLOR ME CRIMINAL

ONE T. REX OVER EASY

THE COCOA COMMOTION

TAKE THE MUMMY AND RUN

And coming soon:

HIGHWAY ROBBERY

Take the Mummy and Run

A CARMEN SANDIEGO™ MYSTERY

by Ellen Weiss & Mel Friedman

Illustrated by S. M. Taggart

*Based on the computer software
created by Brøderbund Software, Inc.*

HarperTrophy®
A Division of HarperCollinsPublishers

Harper Trophy® is a registered trademark of
HarperCollins Publishers Inc.

Take the Mummy and Run

Copyright © 1997 by Brøderbund Software, Inc.
All rights reserved. No part of this book may be used or
reproduced in any manner whatsoever without written permission except in
the case of brief quotations embodied in critical articles and reviews.
Printed in the United States of America. For information address
HarperCollins Children's Books, a division of HarperCollins Publishers,
10 East 53rd Street, New York, NY 10022.

Library of Congress Cataloging-in-Publication Data
Weiss, Ellen 1949–
Take the mummy and run / by Ellen Weiss and Mel Friedman ; illustrated
by S. M. Taggart
    p.   cm. (A Carmen Sandiego mystery)
"Based on the computer software created by Brøderbund Software, Inc."
Summary: When King Tut's mummy vanishes while being sent from Egypt
to a special exhibition in St. Petersburg, Russia, ACME detectives Ben and
Maya set out to find the thief.
    ISBN 0-06-440664-4
    [1. Mystery and detective stories.] I. Friedman, Mel. II. Taggart, S. M., ill.
III. Title. IV. Series.
PZ7.W4475Tak 1997   97-18057
[Fic]—dc21   CIP
                                                                    AC

Typography by Steve Scott
1   2   3   4   5   6   7   8   9   10
❖
First Edition

Visit us on the World Wide Web!
http://www.harperchildrens.com

To Lucas Maximillian
with love

Prologue
St. Petersburg, Russia

As the gleaming white Egyptian steamer eased into its berth in St. Petersburg harbor, the crowd of Russians waiting on the pier burst into applause. After months of careful planning, the *Cairo Calyph* had finally arrived.

The ship wasn't carrying just any cargo. Its hold was filled with ancient treasures from the tomb of King Tutankhamen, including the gold coffin in which King Tut's mummy had lain for nearly three thousand years. These amazing objects had been allowed outside Egypt only a few times. Now they had made the long voyage to Russia for a special exhibition at St. Petersburg's world-famous Hermitage Museum.

Of all the Russians gathered on the pier,

Alexander Nyetsky was perhaps the most excited. Nyetsky was St. Petersburg's Deputy Director of Old, Dusty, and Interesting Things. He, more than anyone else, had been responsible for making the Tut exhibition happen. If the show went well, he was sure to get a promotion.

Nyetsky watched as the gangplank descended and a party of about a dozen Egyptian officials filed ashore. He rushed over to greet them.

"Helloing to you!" he called in broken English—the only language both the Russians and Egyptians could understand. "I am Alexander Nyetsky. I hope you are remembering my name. This exhibit is total my responsibleness. Please being not to worry."

The Egyptians nodded politely and smiled.

"Okay," said Nyetsky, clapping his hands together. "Let us getting going." He pulled a large red handkerchief from his pocket and waved it over his head. This was the signal for the dockworkers to begin unloading the ship.

Soon the wharf was bustling with activity. Cranes whirred. Chains clanked. Trucks groaned under the weight of the huge metal crates that contained the riches of King Tut. And the man in charge of the Egyptian group strolled about with

his video camera, recording the whole historic event to show his friends back home at the museum in Cairo.

At noon the last crate rose from the hold of the *Cairo Calyph* and swung out over the pier. Nyetsky beamed proudly. The unloading had gone off without a hitch. He could almost hear the words of praise coming from his boss.

But just as he was turning to speak with some Egyptians, Nyetsky heard a loud snap. Out of the corner of his eye he caught sight of a huge crate plummeting earthward. Above it was a crane with a dangling chain.

"Aieeyeeee!" shrieked the Egyptians as the container smashed into an empty section of the pier.

"Oyyyyyyy!" wailed Nyetsky as he realized that his dreams of a better job were gone forever.

Three Egyptians dashed to the spot and began clawing at the crate. "This is number forty-five!" one yelled. "King Tut's mummy is inside! We must get it open and check for damage." Nyetsky got a hammer and started pounding on the lock. Others joined in until the crate looked like a sugar cube swarming with ants. Everyone was getting into everyone else's way. No one was getting anywhere.

Just then a strong and clear voice boomed out from the ship.

"Stand back!"

The crowd fell silent as a paunchy figure with coal-black eyes and a handlebar mustache waddled down the gangplank and over to the crate. He was wearing an Australian bush hat, a khaki explorer's outfit, and a brown leather jacket. A curled whip dangled from his belt. He pulled a red lollipop from his mouth and pointed it accusingly at Nyetsky and the Egyptians. "You keep on banging like that," he said, "and you'll turn that old mummy into a pile of sawdust. You'd better let an expert take charge." He took a long, squiggly nail from his hatband and inserted it into the lock. The door popped open a few inches, and the man with the mustache shone a flashlight inside.

Nyetsky turned to the Egyptian man standing next to him. "Excusing, please," he whispered. "Who is big guy there?"

The Egyptian appeared surprised. "You mean you don't know? That's Jersey Jones, the famous explorer."

"Oh," said Nyetsky sheepishly. "This is name I think I'm hearing before. Is this same Jones as—?"

5

"Shhh!" the Egyptian said. "He's going to say something."

Jersey Jones turned to the group with a grave expression on his face.

"What is it?" the Egyptian asked anxiously. "Is the mummy okay?"

Jersey shook his head. "Wish I could say so. You'd better see this for yourself." He threw the crate door wide open. A gasp went up from the crowd. The container was empty! The mummy and its gold coffin had vanished!

"Tut's gone?" the Egyptian cried in disbelief.

"The proper word is *stolen*," corrected Jersey.

"Who is it could be doing such a thing?" Nyetsky asked, feeling faint.

"I've got a pretty good idea," Jersey said. "The person who stole King Tut's mummy seems to have left a business card. I found this inside the crate." He held up a small piece of paper with a weird drawing on it:

"What does it mean?" someone asked.

Jersey frowned. "It means big trouble. This is someone's name, written in ancient Egyptian hieroglyphics. And that person's name is *Carmen*—as in Carmen Sandiego."

1

San Francisco, California, USA

The two-person hoversled hurtled down the mountain. It skimmed over an ice patch, hopped a row of hedges, and headed straight for a boulder a hundred yards down the slope.

"Watch this!" shouted the girl at the controls, her brown eyes flashing with excitement.

"Oh, no, not again," groaned the boy in the seat behind her. He took a deep breath and tightened his grip on the safety bar.

With a mischievous laugh, the girl gunned the engine. The sled picked up speed, leaving blustery clouds of snow behind it.

The boulder lay dead ahead. It was looming larger by the second.

"Maybe we should turn now, Maya," the boy suggested.

"Just relax, Ben," the girl said. "There's nothing to be scared of."

The trail dipped suddenly. Ben felt his stomach do flip-flops. "Next time your aunt Velma buys us tickets to go someplace," he said, "remind me not to come."

Maya smiled. Ben was her best friend in the whole world. They'd grown up together on the same block in San Francisco. And even though Ben was eleven and she was nine, he never seemed to mind that she was always out in front. But Maya also knew that Ben was much braver than he thought. She'd seen evidence of his courage time and time again when they'd been out on special assignment for her aunt Velma.

Aunt Velma—known to everybody else as The Chief—was the head of ACME CrimeNet, the world-famous crime-fighting organization. Maya and Ben were her youngest and brightest detectives. When the two weren't in school or just hanging out on the block like normal kids, they were racing around the globe in hot pursuit of the greatest criminal mind of all time: Carmen Sandiego. Two months ago, they'd come closer than anybody ever had to capturing this elusive thief. Carmen had stolen the keys to the locks on the Panama Canal. No ship could get in or out. There was instant gridlock in the sea-lanes of the western hemisphere. Maya and Ben had tracked Carmen from the jungles of Central America to the fjords of Norway. Finally they found the stolen goods cleverly hidden among the Florida Keys. Unfortunately, Carmen had managed to slip away in a submarine at the last instant. But everyone agreed that Maya and Ben's sleuthing had been brilliant. The Chief was so pleased that she'd rewarded them with two tickets to Virtual Reality Fun Park.

Now Ben was wishing that she'd offered them two tickets to the aquarium instead.

"Turn, Maya, turn!" he cried as the sled raced toward the rock.

Maya slammed the gearshift to "maxlift" and yanked back on the wheel. The sled soared gracefully over the boulder with inches to spare. Then it did a lazy loop in the air before Maya set it down safely at the bottom of the hill.

"Cool ride, huh?" Maya said. She took off her virtual-reality goggles and climbed out of the hoversled simulator. "You know, we were never in any real danger. It was only an illusion."

"More like a nightmare," Ben said as he staggered out of his seat.

They were standing in a large room with a wind machine and an artificial snowmaker. As their eyes became accustomed to the light, they discovered they were not alone. They could see, beside the wind machine, a bald man in a gray uniform perched atop a unicycle. He was struggling to maintain his balance.

"Ahem!" said the man.

Ben rubbed his eyes. "Now I'm really seeing things."

Maya blinked. "Yul?" she addressed the unicyclist. "Is that you?"

"Yul B. Gowen, at your service," the bald man replied with a smile. "If you need a travel plan, I'm your man."

Ben winced. Yul was ACME's special agent in charge of transportation and lodging. He was very good at his job, but very bad at his jokes.

"What are you doing here?" Ben asked, wiping snowflakes from his glasses.

"Something's come up," Yul said. "The Chief wants you back at headquarters—ASAP!"

"We just got here," moaned Maya. "We haven't done the virtual sky dive yet."

Ben gave Maya a dark look. "Oh, no. You're not getting me on that one. I like my lunch right where it is."

Yul pedaled closer. "I'm afraid there's no time to lose, kids," he said, lowering his voice to a whisper. "The Chief has declared a *priority one* emergency."

Maya's pretty brown eyes widened. "Wow! This must really be big. ACME's never gone to *priority one* before." She and Ben exchanged looks. They knew what they had to do.

"We're ready to go," they said in unison.

"Er—Yul, there's just one thing," Ben said. "Could you tell me what you're doing on that unicycle?"

"Oh, didn't you know?" Yul said. "ACME's in a budget crunch. The Chief wants us to make do with less. So I cut up a bunch of our bicycles and turned them into unicycles. Now we've got twice the fleet. The only problem is," he said, nearly falling over, "they're impossible to ride."

Ben glanced at Maya and rolled his eyes.

"By the way," Yul said, "there are two unicycles waiting for you outside."

"No, thanks," said Ben. "We'll take the bus."

2
San Francisco, California, USA

The Chief received them in her spacious office at ACME headquarters. Maya loved her aunt's office. It had a breathtaking view of the Golden Gate Bridge. In one corner stood an old jukebox that only played tunes from the 1960s. And all along the oak-paneled walls were hundreds of snapshots of presidents and kings and legendary ACME detectives who had made it into the Crimestoppers' Hall of Fame.

As a toddler, Maya had spent many happy hours playing in this office. Aunt Velma was just Aunt Velma back then. Now, when Maya entered this room, she had to stop and remind herself that Aunt Velma was also The Chief of ACME, and her boss.

The Chief motioned them to sit down beside her desk. Her eyes looked tired, as if she hadn't had much sleep.

"What do you know about this?" she asked, handing Maya and Ben a photograph. The picture was of a golden coffin shaped like a person. A young boy's face was carved into the lid. And it was decorated with intricate designs of animals and winged creatures.

"It's totally awesome," Ben said. "But I don't have a clue what it is."

"How about you, Maya?" The Chief asked.

Maya twirled a braid around one finger and thought. "Well, it looks kind of Egyptian," she said. "And only kings could afford gold. So I'd guess this was the coffin of a pharaoh. Maybe even King Tut."

"Right you are," said The Chief. "And inside the coffin is the mummy of King Tut himself."

"Gosh," Ben exclaimed. "A real live mummy?"

"No, actually," The Chief said dryly. "A really dead one."

Maya passed the photo back. "I don't get it, Chief. Why the ancient history lesson?"

The Chief's expression grew somber. "Because King Tut's coffin and mummy have been stolen."

Maya and Ben were speechless.

"Take a look at this, gumshoes," The Chief said, pressing a button on her desk. The paneling on one wall rolled away, revealing a huge video screen. "Someone shot this videotape in St. Petersburg, Russia, yesterday. It was beamed to us by satellite, after the theft was discovered. Pay attention to the crane on the right."

Maya and Ben watched with horror as the awful scene unfolded before their eyes. The accident. The panic to open the crate. The appearance of the roly-poly, lollipop-sucking figure. The shocking discovery that the crate was empty.

"How could the mummy get stolen?" Ben asked. "That crate looked harder to crack than a bank vault."

"It was," said The Chief, pausing the tape. "I can vouch for that, because ACME's Crime Prevention Labs made it."

Ben was stunned. "You mean, somebody broke into one of *our* high-tech security crates?"

The Chief nodded gravely. "But the culprit wasn't just anybody," she said.

"Well, there's only one person I know smart enough to pull that off," Ben said.

"Carmen Sandiego!" shouted Maya.

"Bingo!" said The Chief. Then she paused the videotape to show the two junior detectives a close-up of the scrap of paper with Carmen's name in hieroglyphics. "I don't know how—or why—Carmen committed this dastardly crime, but Tut's mummy and coffin must be recovered."

As The Chief spoke, she opened one of her desk drawers and withdrew a thermos bottle and three small glasses. Maya and Ben gave each other a puzzled look.

"ACME's reputation is on the line here," The Chief went on. "That's why I'm assigning my two best agents to the case." She unscrewed the cap on the thermos.

"You mean detectives Katz and Doggs?" Ben said.

"No," The Chief said, filling the glasses with a thick, purplish-red liquid. "I mean you two."

Maya and Ben broke into huge smiles. The Chief was giving them another chance to take on Carmen. This time the queen of crime wouldn't get away.

"When do we leave?" Maya said excitedly.

"Hold on," said Ben. "First I want to know *where* we're going. Do I need to pack sweaters or shorts?"

"Yul has made all the arrangements," The Chief replied. "You'll fly to St. Petersburg tonight. I want you to interview the man who opened the crate—Jersey Jones."

"Is he an ACME operative?" Ben asked.

"No," The Chief said. "But he's an expert on King Tut. And a big-time explorer. I'm told he can speak twenty-five languages. You might want to team up with him. He could prove extremely useful."

"How much time do we have to find Tut?" Maya asked.

The Chief stared straight into Maya's eyes. "Not much, I'm afraid. The Tut exhibition opens on August first. The Egyptians want the mummy back by then—or else."

"Or else what?" said Maya.

"Or else they'll sue us. It *was* our crate, don't forget. I'd say it could be in the neighborhood of forty-five million dollars."

Ben's jaw dropped. "Ay-yi-yi," he croaked.

"But Chief—that gives us only fifteen days!" Maya said.

"I know," The Chief said wearily. "But that's all we have. If the Egyptians sue us, we'll be ruined." She handed Maya and Ben each a glass of the purplish drink.

"What's this?" Ben asked, making a face.

"Borscht," The Chief answered. "It's like Russian tomato soup—only it's made from beets. You'd better get used to it. You'll be drinking a lot of it in St. Petersburg." The Chief raised her glass in a toast. "Here's to a successful mission."

"And to nabbing Carmen," added Maya.

With that, the three of them downed their glasses of borscht.

Ben tried hard not to hate it.

IN A RUBY-RED JET STREAKING HIGH OVER THE MEDITERRANEAN SEA . . .

What a stroke of good luck! The satellite transmission of that video wasn't scrambled. Picking up the signal was as easy as pie. Now I've got a copy of the tape too. I guess it won't be long before ACME sends someone out to catch me. Only this time, the joke's on both of us. Because I didn't steal that mummy. And I didn't authorize any of my henchpeople to do it either. I never rob museum treasures. It's totally against my principles. I steal only for the game—for the joy of pitting my wits against the world's greatest crime-stoppers. Someone's trying to frame me. But who? Someone in my own gang? I'd better set a course for St. Petersburg. I've got some sleuthing of my own to do.

3

St. Petersburg, Russia

A chilly gust of wind blew off the river. Maya gave a shiver and buttoned up her jean jacket.

"Where is he?" she asked, glancing anxiously at her watch. "We've been here for over an hour. You're sure we're in the right place?"

"Positive," Ben said. "Do you want me to check the Sender again?"

Maya nodded. "Maybe I input the map data wrong. You know how I am with computers."

Ben grinned. It was true that Maya was pretty hopeless as far as computers were concerned. She made up for it by being a genius when it came to geography and history.

He reached into his knapsack and fished out the Ultra-Secret Sender. The Sender was ACME's most advanced high-tech gadget. Packed in a case the size of a Walkman was a combination super-computer, videophone, and camcorder. It also featured a fax, a universal decoder, and high-speed access to the Internet and ACME's CrimeNet database. The Ultra-Secret Sender was an ACME agent's lifeline. No smart detective would ever leave home without one.

Ben flipped up the lid on his Sender, and a tiny computer screen blinked on. In the base opposite the screen was a miniature keyboard with dozens of coded buttons. Ben's fingers flew skillfully over the keyboard as if he were playing an old and familiar instrument. Soon the words RETRIEVING E-MAIL appeared in the center of the glowing blue screen.

"Here it is," Ben said, showing Maya. "This is the E-mail Jersey Jones sent us right after we landed."

Maya read it again:

DEAR BEN AND MAYA:
WELCOME TO ST. PETERSBURG! YOUR CHIEF
TOLD ME YOU WERE ON THE CASE. BULLY!
WILL MEET YOU AT THE BRONZE
HORSEMAN, 9 P.M. TELL NO ONE. THE

STREETS HAVE MANY EARS. I HAVE
IMPORTANT NEWS ABOUT THE LADY IN RED.
REGARDS,
JERSEY JONES, WORLD EXPLORER EXTRAORDINAIRE

Maya scratched her head. "You have to admit, Ben. This isn't the clearest note we've ever received. We could have gone to the wrong place. For all we know, the Bronze Horseman could be a restaurant."

"I don't think so," Ben said. "For once I think you input the data right. Look." He pressed a few buttons on the Sender and called up a street map of St. Petersburg. Then he zoomed in on a spot labeled BRONZE HORSEMAN. The picture on the screen was of a large bronze statue of a man on a horse. The rider was staring watchfully out over the Neva River. The horse was rearing up and trampling on a snake.

Maya's gaze shifted from the Sender to the public square where they were standing. Everything seemed to match the picture perfectly. A few yards away was the same statue of the mighty horseman.

"Okay," Maya said. "So we got the location right. But that still doesn't answer the big question. Where's Jersey Jones? I'm starting to get worried."

"About what?"

Maya eyed a group of sightseers lingering by the statue. When they'd passed, she said, "Well, his message seemed kind of secretive. I mean, he told us to make sure nobody knew about this meeting."

"Right," agreed Ben.

"And he didn't refer to Carmen by name."

"That's right!" Ben said. "He called her 'the Lady in Red.' Maybe he was afraid somebody might be reading our E-mail."

"Exactly. So I'm wondering if something could have happened to him."

"Gosh!" exclaimed Ben. "I hope not."

"No need to worry!" came a thunderous voice from behind the statue.

Ben was so startled that he dropped the Sender. Only Maya's quick reflexes saved it from slamming to the ground. As she slipped the Sender back into Ben's knapsack for safekeeping, a stocky man in an explorer's outfit emerged from the shadows.

"Don't bother introducing yourselves," the man said. "I know who you are. They call me Jones— Jersey Jones."

"Do you always make surprise entrances like

23

this?" Maya asked, recalling the scene on the docks in The Chief's video.

Jersey smiled. "Actually, I've been here for a while."

"You have?" Ben said in amazement. "How come we didn't see you?" He gazed around the flat, open square. "There's no place to hide."

"Trade secret, son," Jersey said. "Something I learned from the pygmies in Africa. Comes in real handy when a lion's on your trail."

"Amazing!" exclaimed Ben admiringly.

"Why didn't you tell us you were here?" Maya asked, feeling a little foolish that she'd been so worried about his safety.

Jersey motioned the two sleuths to come in closer. "I had to see if you were being followed."

"Followed? By whom?" Maya said.

"Why—V.I.L.E. operatives, of course," the explorer replied. "First they were in Egypt, and now they're here in Russia."

At the mention of the Villains' International League of Evil, Maya's and Ben's ears pricked up. V.I.L.E. was the name of Carmen Sandiego's infamous gang of criminals. No police lineup ever held a more shifty-eyed, fast-talking bunch of rogues.

"What do you know about V.I.L.E. and the King Tut heist?" Maya inquired.

Jersey went rooting around in his pockets. Maya thought he was looking for information. Instead, he pulled out a big chocolate bar and bit off a piece. "I don't know about you children," he said between chews, "but I'm hungrier than a rhino in the dry season. Why don't we all go someplace private and eat? Then I'll tell you everything I know."

Maya immediately observed two things. First, Jersey didn't offer to share his candy bar. (Not that she wanted a bite.) And second, he addressed them as "children." Nobody called her a child anymore, at least not at work. As a trained crime-fighting professional, Maya felt she was entitled to greater respect. Jersey Jones might be a "world explorer extraordinaire," she grumbled to herself, but he could use a few lessons in manners.

Jersey led them along a beautiful canal toward the heart of St. Petersburg. "This whole city was a swamp three hundred years ago," he said with a sweep of his arm. "Then Peter the Great came along and built his new capital here."

"Peter the Who?" Ben asked.

"Peter the Great, son," repeated Jersey. "One of Russia's most famous rulers. Remember that statue where we met?"

"You mean the Bronze Horseman?"

Jersey nodded. "That's old Peter up there in the saddle. And did you spot the snake under his horse's hooves?"

"Uh-huh," Ben said.

"Well, that critter is supposed to represent his enemies."

"Wow, Jersey," Ben said. "You know *so* much."

"Oh, you just pick things up when you've been everywhere and done everything," he said with a yawn.

At the restaurant Jersey ordered a round of borscht and a plate of blintzes and sour cream for everyone. The food came quickly. The blintzes were thin, rolled pancakes filled with fruit jams and cheese. Jersey cleared a small space on the table and plopped his hat down in the middle.

"As you know," he began, "I'm the world's greatest living expert on King Tut. So the Egyptians quite naturally hired me to make sure that old pile of bones got to St. Petersburg okay." He paused momentarily and pulled a long, squiggly nail from his hatband. "Recognize this?" he asked.

Maya and Ben shook their heads no.

"Just looks like an old, bent nail, huh?" Jersey continued. "But it's not. It's the master key to the Tut security crates. Made of a tungsten-dilerium alloy—strongest metal known to man. There are only three of these keys in existence. Your Chief's got one. I've got another—I keep it on my person at all times. And the head of the Cairo museum had the third."

"Had?" remarked Ben, raising an eyebrow.

"That's right, son—had. That third key was stolen the day before the *Cairo Calyph* set sail for Russia."

"Has it been recovered?" Maya asked.

Jersey frowned. "I'm afraid not," he said. "But maybe this will help." He removed a crumpled piece of paper from a tiny pocket inside his hat. On it were scrawled two names: *Fast Eddie B.* and *Sarah Nade.*

The names registered like bolts of lightning.

"They're both V.I.L.E. operatives!" Ben exclaimed.

"Two of Carmen's best," added Maya gravely. She gave Jersey a searching look. "What do Fast Eddie B. and Sarah Nade have to do with the missing mummy?"

Jersey slipped the key back into his hatband. "Well, on the day the third key disappeared," he said, "they were both seen in Cairo."

"By whom?" Ben probed, typing away madly on the Sender.

"Friends of mine in the Egyptian police. They passed the word on to me."

Maya eyes lit up. "Of course!" she squealed. "Why didn't I think of that before? Cairo is one of Carmen's secret bases. Maybe Sarah or Fast Eddie hid out there, stole the key, then snatched the mummy before it left Cairo!"

Jersey put his hat back on, and continued eating his blintzes. Maya was astounded at how much food the man could stuff into his mouth while still talking. "There's only one problem with that theory," he said. "Tut wasn't stolen in Cairo. I know. I loaded him into the crate myself. Then I watched that crate like a hawk until it was safely on the ship."

Maya's face fell. "Rats!" she said. "I thought I had it all figured out."

"Oh, c'mon, Maya," Ben teased. "Since when has Carmen ever made anything easy for us?"

"I suppose you've got a better idea?" Maya said with a pout.

"Actually, I do," Ben said. "I think Tut was stolen off the ship—somewhere between Cairo and here. Sarah or Fast Eddie could have stowed away onboard. Then they could have unlocked the crate, removed the coffin, and lowered it overboard onto a waiting sub. Carmen's got a whole fleet of them."

"My conclusion exactly," gurgled Jersey as he washed down his last bite of blintz with a full pitcher of borscht.

Ben furrowed his brow in thought. "The big question is, where do we start looking? There's thousands of miles of sea between here and Cairo. Wait a minute," he said, snapping his fingers. "Jersey—you said something before about V.I.L.E. operatives in St. Petersburg. What did you mean?"

Jersey had already turned his attention to the bowl of sour cream. He was emptying it out onto his plate. "Well, when I signed in at my hotel," he said, "I couldn't help noticing that there were two other English signatures on the page."

"Don't tell me," Ben said. "Fast Eddie B. and Sarah Nade."

Jersey nodded his head and said, "You're sharper than Cleopatra's Needle, boy."

Maya grew excited. "That means the robbery

probably took place close to here. So maybe there's still time to get the mummy back before they leave town."

"Yes!" cried Ben.

Meanwhile, Jersey was hungrily eyeing Ben's half-eaten blintzes. "You're not going to finish these, are you, son?" he said. "Hope you don't mind if I help myself." In an instant Jersey had reached for Ben's plate and was scarfing down his food. And after the explorer had polished off Ben's meal, he finished Maya's leftovers.

"Yuck," muttered Maya under her breath. She glanced at Ben to see if he was as grossed out as she was. But Ben seemed as cheerful as ever.

After Maya and Ben had paid the check, they arranged with Jersey to meet again tomorrow. Then they headed back toward their hotel, strolling along a winding canal.

"I don't care if Jersey Jones is a world-famous expert," Maya said. "I think he's icky."

"Well, maybe his table manners aren't great," said Ben. "But he's really smart. He's going to be a big help in this case."

It was nearly midnight, but the sky was bright with sunlight. People still filled the streets and outdoor cafés. Musicians on the sidewalks were

31

playing songs and a group of jugglers was delighting a crowd in front of a church.

"What gives?" said Ben. "Am I crazy—or did the sun forget to go down?"

Maya laughed. "You're not crazy," she said. "You're just totally clueless about geography. St. Petersburg is so far north that the sun never really sets in summer. It's light out for twenty-four hours. The Russians call it 'white night.' "

"That's so cool," Ben said as they arrived at their hotel. "It also gives us an edge tomorrow."

"How's that?" asked Maya.

"It means that if Fast Eddie B. and Sarah Nade are still in this city, they'll have no place to hide."

4
St. Petersburg, Russia

"**H**elp!" screeched Maya. "This thing's going berserk!" Maya sat cross-legged on the bed and watched helplessly as the Sender printed out an endless stream of gobbledygook. "How do I shut it off?"

Ben looked up from his chair. "Don't panic, Maya," he said, dashing to the rescue.

"It hates me. I know it hates me. It's doing this on purpose!" Maya's legs were covered with printer paper.

"Hmm," said Ben, examining a few inches of the printout. "Very interesting." The printout read:

FAST EDDIE B.: IGLOX SPLUT CHEWYR

SQUILLIUM IRET. NIPPY EARWET NISH.

He paused and squinted extra hard. "Hey, I'm having trouble with the next line," he said. "How would you pronounce this?" He handed the paper to Maya. The line read:

ÓPⱯ⸸ IRΘᎧ$O FÖNØⵁB, ⱯÖLÜ ÑOR.

Maya squinted at it too, and Ben burst out laughing. "This must be a new ACME code," he giggled.

"Funny. Very funny," Maya said, fuming. "Would you ple-e-e-a-se get me out of this program?"

"Easy," Ben said. "Just hit 'escape,' then 'alt' and 'shift' together, then 'F9,' 'subtext,' and 'defcon3.'"

"Easy for you," Maya grumped as she executed Ben's commands. With what sounded like an electronic burp, the runaway program halted. "Here," she said, handing Ben the Sender. "*You* can get the profiles on Fast Eddie B. and Sarah Nade. *I'm* calling room service for breakfast."

While Maya went for the telephone, Ben punched a few keys, and the microprinter in the case began spitting out information without mishap. "Got it!" Ben called.

"Great!" said Maya, placing her hand over the

mouthpiece of the phone. "This menu is all in Russian. So I ordered us two deluxe specials plus something called *odali* and something called *shchi boyarski*."

"Okay," Ben replied warily. "Just as long as it's not borscht."

Minutes later Ben was staring at a plate of smoked eel and fish eggs. "Yuck!" he said. "Next time, remind me to use the Sender to translate the menu *before* we order."

"Lighten up," Maya said, grinning. "It's not so bad once you get used to it. I sorta like my cabbage soup."

Ben grimaced. "I'll stick with the *odali*," he said. "Pancakes are pancakes all over the world."

After Maya finished her meal, she said, "Now, you want to show me what you got on Fast Eddie and Sarah?"

Ben handed Maya the printout. It read:

> **FAST EDDIE B.** 5′7″ TALL, BLACK HAIR, BROWN EYES, MUSTACHE, WELL DRESSED. WORLD-CLASS CROQUET PLAYER. LIKES MEXICAN FOOD. DRIVES CONVERTIBLE.

SARAH NADE. 5'4½" TALL, BLOND HAIR, GRAY EYES, SCAR BELOW RIGHT EAR IN SHAPE OF NEW JERSEY. MOONLIGHTS AS LEAD SINGER FOR HAWAIIAN PUNK BAND THE SARCASTIC FRINGEHEADS. LIKES CHINESE FOOD, A NUT FOR TV SOAP OPERAS. DRIVES LIMOUSINE EQUIPPED WITH TV SATELLITE DISH.

"This everything?" Maya asked.

"I'm not sure," Ben said. "CrimeNet's circuits were jammed."

"It's good enough for now," Maya said. "We can access the full dossiers later."

"What's our next move?" he asked.

Maya slipped on her fanny pack. "Let's head over to Jersey's hotel. I'd like to ask the manager there a few questions about our prime suspects."

The manager of the Neva Goodinuff Hotel was sorting mail behind the desk when the two ACME detectives arrived.

"Excuse me," Ben began. "Do you speak English?"

"Oh, you are Americans!" exclaimed the manager. "I am loving Americans. You are knowing Madonna?"

"Uh, no—not personally," Ben said.

"Tom Cruise?"

"No, sorry."

"Too bad," the manager said. "I am loving Madonna and Tom Cruise."

"Er—that's great," Ben said. "We do too."

The manager put the mail down. "Now, how may I be helping you?"

Maya and Ben showed him their ACME badges and explained why they had come.

"Oh, my miniature American friends," he said. "I'm afraid you are coming too late. Ms. Nade has—how you say?—made a powder last night."

"You mean, she *took* a powder?" Maya ventured.

"You are saying the words right out of my mouth," the manager replied. "Ms. Nade is going in big rush. Too late, in fact, to be getting this." He reached under the desk and pulled out a small package the size of a shoe box. It was gift wrapped in beautiful red-and-gold paper. "It was coming for her this morning. Please to take it with you if you like."

"I don't know if we should," said Maya.

"It might be evidence," Ben argued. "If not, we'll see Sarah gets it."

Maya relented. "All right," she said to the manager. "We'll take it."

"Okeydokey," he said cheerily.

"You wouldn't happen to know where Ms. Nade went?" Ben said.

"I am sorry, I do not."

"Could you tell us if Fast Eddie B. left with her?" asked Maya.

The manager checked the guest book. "No. This I am saying positively. Mr. B. is not checking out. In fact," he said, pointing with his finger, "there he is now."

Maya and Ben spun around and saw an elegantly dressed man in a white linen suit slinking out the main entrance. He was sneaking a backward glance at Maya and Ben.

"There he goes! C'mon!" cried Maya, grabbing Ben's arm and hauling him toward the door.

"Wait, my little Yankee radishes, come back . . ." shouted the manager. "Are you knowing Bill Cosby? I am loving Bill Cosby."

Maya and Ben raced outside. Fast Eddie B. glanced back over his shoulder. When he saw Ben and Maya following him, a look of panic swept across his face. Wheeling, he sprinted toward the waterfront.

"Stop, Fast Eddie!" yelled Maya. "We're ACME agents. We want to ask you a few questions."

Fast Eddie wasn't in the mood for a chat. He fled down an alley leading toward the piers.

Maya and Ben gave chase. At the end of the alley they skidded to a stop. Maya scratched her head. They were standing on an empty dock. Fast Eddie was nowhere in sight.

Ben leaned against the wall to catch his breath. "Rats! He gave us the slip."

Maya was hardly sweating. "Listen," she said. "Did you hear that?"

Ben wiped the steam off his glasses with his shirttail. "You mean, my lungs exploding?"

"No, *that*."

Now Ben heard it too. It was the sound of an outboard motor revving up. It was coming from the other side of the dock.

"No time to lose!" Maya cried. "Follow me."

"You've got to be kidding," Ben groaned. Replacing his half-fogged glasses, he ran after Maya. As they reached the edge of the dock, they saw Fast Eddie in a motorboat heading out into the open river.

Maya looked wildly about. Suddenly she had

an idea. "We'll take that boat," she said.

"What boat?" said Ben, panting hard.

"That one—the hydrofoil."

Ben looked and saw a sleek bullet-shaped tourist boat moored to the dock. Nobody was on it.

"Oh, no, Maya. We can't borrow that boat," Ben said. "You don't know how to drive a hydrofoil."

"How hard could it be?" Maya replied. "It probably handles like a hoversled."

Ben gulped. "That's what I was afraid of."

Maya had already scampered aboard. "C'mon, this is our big chance!" she yelled. "You want to catch Fast Eddie—or what?"

Soon the hydrofoil, with Maya at the wheel, was slicing through the gray waves of the Neva River. They were leaving the city behind.

Seeing the ACME agents gaining on him, Fast Eddie stepped on the gas. He swerved around a tiny island and roared under a low-lying bridge.

"Bet he thinks we're gonna slow down to see if we can make it under that bridge," Maya said. "His boat is a lot lower than ours."

Ben gasped. "You mean, we're not going to make it under?"

"Doubtful," Maya replied.

Ben's face whitened. He pulled out his Sender and began typing like a maniac.

"What are you doing?" Maya asked.

"Writing my will. I calculate I've got twenty-seven seconds to fax it to The Chief before you turn us into Silly Putty."

"How about figuring wave patterns, instead?" Maya said. "If we can shoot ahead of the next wave, there's a good chance we can slip through."

"I get it," Ben said excitedly. "We position the boat *between* the waves—so the crests don't lift us up!"

"Exactly!"

In the distance, Maya could see Fast Eddie's boat curving toward shore. The bridge was almost upon them. "I've got to speed up now," she shouted. "How much faster to beat the waves?"

Ben's hand shook as he calculated the numbers on the Sender. "Try three point five knots!" he cried.

"Roger—up three point five!" Maya said, opening the throttle. "Here we go-o-o-o. . . ."

Ben closed his eyes as the hydrofoil shot into the darkness under the bridge. When he opened them, he noticed three things. He wasn't in heaven. The boat was still in one piece. And Maya was giving him the thumbs-up sign.

"You did it, Ben!" she exclaimed. "You got us through. Now nothing can stop us from nabbing Fast Eddie!"

In a matter of minutes, Fast Eddie was scrambling out of his boat and onto the shore, with Maya and Ben in hot pursuit. They were at the bottom of a path that led up a steep hill. Above them was a maze of gardens and fountains with a beautiful, huge palace on the hilltop.

Maya did a double take. "I know what this place is!" she said, already breathing hard from the climb. "This is the summer palace of that guy Jersey was telling us about, Peter the Great. We had a picture of it in my geography book last year."

"Did they have to build it on such a high hill?" panted Ben.

They could see Fast Eddie up ahead, darting in and out of the garden paths. He was trying to lose them.

Maya and Ben were too smart for him, though. They split up and circled around behind him. Fast Eddie was fast, but Maya and Ben were faster. Eddie kept climbing up the path, thinking he'd left Ben and Maya far behind. But instead, they were closing in on him.

At the last second, Maya leaped out from behind a hedge. "Boo!" she yelled.

Fast Eddie was so startled that he tripped over his shoelaces and fell headfirst into a moat.

"Now see what you've done!" Fast Eddie spluttered. "My suit—it's ruined!" He retrieved his beret from a lily pad, and a little frog hopped out. "I demand an explanation for this . . . this outrage!"

Ben helped the dripping man up. "If anybody's got some explaining to do," he said sharply, "it's you, Fast Eddie! We know you were in Cairo recently. What do you know about King Tut's mummy?"

"She makes him brush his teeth every day," Fast Eddie said with a guffaw.

"Put a lid on it, Eddie," Maya said curtly. "You're in big trouble. The Cairo police—"

"Wait a minute," Eddie cut in. "You're not going to pin that one on me. Those mallets were just lying there on the ground in front of the Sphinx. They weren't anybody's. So I took them."

"Huh?" said Maya, looking puzzled. "What are you talking about?"

"You know, the croquet mallets. I never saw such beauties in my life. Hand painted. Solid mahogany. Silver handles. Genuine antiques."

"You mean you stole—"

"*Found,*" corrected Fast Eddie.

"*Found* some croquet mallets, and you thought we were chasing you because of that?"

Now it was Fast Eddie's turn to be surprised. "You weren't?"

Ben and Maya shook their heads. "We're looking for the person who stole King Tut's mummy."

Fast Eddie gave them a horrified look. "Hey— I'm no mummy snatcher. They give me the creeps."

"How do we know you're telling the truth?" Maya said.

"Simple," the thief said. "Just check your files. I always leave a diamond stickpin at the scene of my crimes."

While Maya guarded Fast Eddie to make sure he didn't flee, Ben tapped into CrimeNet.

"His story checks out," Ben reported presently. "CrimeNet confirms that he never commits a crime without leaving a stickpin behind. And no stickpin was found in or near King Tut's crate."

Maya wasn't satisfied. "I still want to know what you were doing in Egypt."

"I was on summer vacation," Fast Eddie said. "Is that a crime?"

"Not usually," Maya replied. "Oh—one more

thing. Do you happen to know the whereabouts of Sarah Nade?"

"Absolutely not!" the thief snapped. "And even if I did, I wouldn't tell you."

Ben and Maya looked at each other. They had reached a dead end.

"Okay," said Ben wearily. "No more questions. You can go now."

As Fast Eddie skipped down the hill, he called back over his shoulder, "I'll send my dry cleaning bill to your Chief."

Over lunch with Jersey, Maya and Ben recounted the disappointing results of their morning. Jersey listened to the details with keen interest, then said, "You forgot only one thing."

"What's that?" Ben asked.

"To open Sarah's package."

"Duh!" Maya blurted out. "How could we be so dumb?"

Ben was already unwrapping the box. Inside was a wooden toy shaped like a bowling pin. A picture of a smiling woman was painted on the outside.

"Aha!" Jersey exclaimed. "A *matryushka* doll."

Maya knew what was it immediately. "I had

one of these when I was little. Just give it a twist, Ben. It'll come apart. You'll find a whole bunch of dolls in there, one inside the other."

Ben opened the dolls one by one until he reached the last one, a tiny figure of a baby. Taped to the baby doll was a small card. Ben read the note aloud:

A REMINDER, DEAR SARAH,
IT'S NOT THE BAHAMAS.
TO BLEND RIGHT IN,
YOU'D BEST TAKE PAJAMAS.
6,000 LONG MILES
YOU'LL BE TRAVELING—AT LEAST!
ON THE WORLD'S LONGEST RAILROAD
TO RULER OF THE EAST.

Ben rolled his eyes. "Don't you just hate poems with clues?"

"They're the pits," agreed Maya.

Jersey was munching on a bag of nacho-flavored pork rinds. "I believe I can help you out," he said. "Have you ever heard of the Trans-Siberian Railroad?"

The name sounded familiar to Maya. "Isn't that the longest railroad in the world?"

"Indeed it is," Jersey said. "It goes all the way

across Russia—from Moscow to the Sea of Japan. Somewhere in the neighborhood of six thousand miles long."

"So that must mean Sarah's on a train to Siberia," Ben reasoned. "Siberia is *definitely* not the Bahamas." He paused. "But I still don't get the pajamas part."

"That's a cinch," Jersey said, munching a greasy pork rind. "The trip through Siberia takes days. Russians often change into their pajamas for the whole journey."

"That leaves one piece to the puzzle," Ben said. "'Ruler of the East.'"

"I think I know that one," interjected Maya. "The last stop on the Trans-Siberian Railroad is Vladivostok. And I know from reading Russian maps that *vostok* means 'east.' So I bet *Ruler of the East* is just English for Vladivostok."

"My hat's off to you, little lady," Jersey said. "You really know your geography."

Maya beamed. Maybe Jersey wasn't so bad after all. "I guess we'd better call Yul B. Gowen," she said. "We've got to book two tickets on Sarah's train."

"Make that three tickets, if you don't mind," Jersey said.

"Yippee!" shouted Ben.

"Siberia—here we come!" cried Maya.

So, it wasn't Fast Eddie who stole the mummy. I knew he didn't do it. I trained him too well. He's one of my most trustworthy henchpeople. Honest. Hardworking. Shares my tastes for convertibles and fine jewelry. A criminal with class. But what about Sarah? Have I been paying her enough attention? Giving her the choice assignments? I bought her a new satellite dish on her birthday. But have I missed something? Is she really happy in my organization? Or is she starting her own?

Make that four tickets for Siberia, Mr. Conductor. Carmen Sandiego is about to hit the rails.

5

The Trans-Siberian Railroad, Central Asia

"**A** *what*?" Maya asked incredulously.
"A spud slide."

Maya stared at Yul's image on the Sender videophone. "This isn't just another one of your corny jokes, is it?"

Yul wasn't smiling. "Negative, kid," he said.

"So, let me get this straight. You're telling me you can't get us on Sarah's train because of a *spud* slide?"

"The biggest ever."

"That's s-p-u-d, as in potatoes?"

"Correct," the ACME travel agent said. "We just got a flash from Moscow. Some idiot farmer left a silo door open, and a zillion potatoes rolled down a hill. Buried the Trans-Siberian Railroad tracks in sixty feet of spuds."

"What about Sarah's train? Did it get stuck?"

Yul shook his head. "Sometimes the bad guys have all the luck. Her train rolled through just before the avalanche. Not a spud touched it."

Maya paced anxiously around her hotel room, Sender in hand. She was all alone with this problem. Ben had gone to pick up Jersey from his hotel.

"Okay, Yul," she said. "We need an alternate plan. Maybe we can intercept her train at one of its stops. When can you get us on the next plane?"

Yul was oddly silent. She tapped the Sender lightly. "Yul, do you read me?" she asked.

"Loud and clear."

"Well?"

"Sorry, Maya, but I can't. With The Chief's budget cuts, the best I can do for you now is a hot-air balloon."

"A hot-air balloon? To catch a train? Now you've really got to be kidding."

Again Yul shook his head. "Wish I were. I can allow you only so many plane rides on this case. The Chief thinks it might be best if you saved some for later."

Maya couldn't believe her ears. "What later?

Yul—we've located our prime suspect! We'll have the mummy back in no time."

"That's just the thing—"

"What?" Maya asked suspiciously. "Yul, is there something you haven't told me?"

"Well, there's been a slight complication to this case."

Maya sat down. "What *kind* of complication?"

"Well, we did a routine scan of our CrimeNet database—"

"Right," said Maya. "It's standard procedure."

"And we discovered that, in addition to Fast Eddie B. and Sarah Nade . . ."

Maya had a strong hunch she wasn't going to like what came next. "Go on," she said.

"There were five other V.I.L.E. operatives sighted in Egypt before the *Cairo Calyph* set sail: Yul B. Sorry, Bjorn Toulouse, Dazzle Annie Nonker, Lady Agatha Wayland, and Bessie Mae Mucho."

Maya felt weak. "So any one of them could be the culprit."

"Unfortunately—yes. But there's good news, too," Yul hastened to add.

Maya frowned. "I don't see how it could be much worse."

"Well, how's this? All five new suspects are in Russia, and they've all bought tickets on the Trans-Siberian Railroad."

"The same train as Sarah?"

"That very one."

Maya's mind whirred away. "So that means when we find Sarah, we find the others. We get all the bad eggs in one basket."

"Precisely," Yul said, breaking into a smile for the first time. "Now, about that hot-air balloon . . ."

The bright-orange hot-air balloon swept silently across a cloudless Russian sky. It flew over farmlands and woods and riverside towns.

Yul had actually set them up quite well, Maya thought. The balloon was equipped with a high-tech navigation system and a small electric propeller for steering. The gondola had fold-down cots and a mini refrigerator, and it was just roomy enough to hold the three travelers and Jersey's bulging bags.

Maya checked their position on the map. They were making excellent time. They'd whizzed past the spud slide hours ago. If the wind held steady, they were bound to overtake Sarah's train by nightfall.

"See those mountains up ahead," she said to Ben. "They're the Urals. Once we cross them, we're not in Europe anymore. We're in Asia."

"Wow, they're incredible," Ben exclaimed as they soared over the wooded slopes. "Hey, Jersey—come look at this," he called over his shoulder. But the only response from the explorer was a muffled snore. Jersey had curled up on his cot, pulled his hat down over his face, and fallen asleep.

Maya switched the balloon to automatic pilot and edged over to Ben's side of the gondola.

"You know, there's something weird about this case," Maya whispered.

"Yeah?" Ben said. "What's that?"

"Well, for as long as we've been tracking Carmen, have you ever known her to steal a historic treasure?"

Ben mulled the question over, then shook his head. "I can't think of a single time."

"Me neither. And that's what I don't get. This crime is totally unlike Carmen. I mean, what's her motive?"

Ben leaned forward and gazed into the distance. "I dunno. She's impossible to figure. Maybe she just wants to embarrass ACME. She once worked for The Chief, remember—before she turned to a life of crime."

"How can I forget? Carmen was a legend. The best of the best. The Chief refuses to take her picture off the wall. Carmen's still up there in the Hall of Fame."

"Maybe Carmen's changed," Ben proposed. "Maybe she's decided she wants the world's greatest art treasures all for herself."

Maya still looked doubtful. "I don't know. If there's one thing that Carmen has—in addition to brains, beauty, wealth, and class—it's character. She never hurts anyone or does anything underhanded. It just doesn't make sense."

"Unless . . . unless someone in V.I.L.E. is acting independently."

"You mean—"

Ben pronounced the words slowly: "I mean a traitor."

"Omigosh, Ben!" Maya exclaimed. "You may be on to something."

That night Maya landed the hot-air balloon in a field beside a train station. It was pitch-dark out. "Here we are," she said.

"Where's here?" Ben asked.

"Krasnoyarsk," replied Maya. "About five hundred miles north of Mongolia. Sarah's train should be arriving in ten minutes."

"My old stomping grounds," Jersey said, reaching for his bags. "Spent a whole year round here looking for the lost gold of Genghis Khan. Lived in a tent. Kept a herd of goats. Made my own frozen yogurt."

"Gosh, Jersey," Ben said. "Did you find the gold?"

"That's what everyone wants to know," Jersey replied, giving Ben a sly wink. "And maybe someday I'll tell you. In the meantime," he said, "you can make yourself useful to old Jersey." He handed Ben his two heaviest suitcases. "How about carrying these for me, son? My ingrown hangnail's acting up."

Ben cheerfully obliged, and the three trudged over to the station, where a crowd of people was milling about the platform.

Maya and Ben couldn't help gawking at the spectacle. Everyone waiting for the train was dressed in pajamas. A few wore silly paper hats made from newspapers. The mood was festive. People were passing around ice cream and cookies and jugs of fruit juice. It looked as if someone

56

had rented the railroad station for a pajama party.

"What's going on?" Ben asked Jersey.

"Quick!" Jersey said to the two youngsters. "There's no time to lose. We've got to change into our pajamas."

"Now?" exclaimed Maya.

"Now," ordered Jersey. "These people are already in their traveling clothes. We should be too, if we don't want to stick out like yaks on a dune."

Minutes later, a long green train with pretty red curtains on its windows chugged into the station, and Ben, Maya, and Jersey—camouflaged in fuzzy pajamas and slippers—hopped aboard.

"I feel real weird walking around like this," Ben said.

"Tell me about it," replied Maya.

The trio found their way to their sleeping car and quietly mapped out their strategy.

"It's too dark to search the train now," Maya said. "Besides, Sarah and the others are probably all asleep. We'll look for them tomorrow morning, when we stop at Irkutsk. Okay?"

"Okay," said Ben.

"Agreed," said Jersey.

Ben put Jersey's suitcases under the explorer's

bunk, then offered to help him with his gym bag too.

"No, thanks, sonny boy," he said. "Nobody touches this one. It's where I stash all my dirty laundry."

Ben laughed. "I've got a wash to do too. I sure hope we solve this case before I run out of socks."

"You and me both," Maya added, squeezing her nose with two fingers.

They all grinned and disappeared into their compartments. Soon, the gentle rocking of the speeding train had them all sound asleep.

The next morning Ben spent five minutes pounding on Jersey's door. "He sleeps like a rock," he finally said to Maya. "I can't wake him."

Maya peered out the train window. The station at Irkutsk had come into view. "We can't wait for Jersey," she said. "In a minute there'll be people all over the place. Let's search the train ourselves."

Ben nodded and handed her a printout from the Sender. On it were mug shots of Sarah and the five other suspects. He slipped a second copy under Jersey's door. Then the two young sleuths began prowling the cars for V.I.L.E. operatives. The train was entering the station as they slid back the door to the dining car.

Sarah Nade was easy to pick out among the diners. She was the only blonde, wearing pajamas decorated with the ugly logo of her punk band, the Sarcastic Fringeheads. As Maya and Ben sneaked closer, she was fussing with a tiny satellite dish perched atop a portable color television set. The picture went all snowy, then locked in crystal clear. Sarah rested her chin on the table and gazed at the screen.

"What she's watching?" Maya whispered.

"Let's find out," Ben whispered back. He tuned the Sender to the same channel and pushed the simultaneous translator button. *"O Genghis, must you go?"* a pretty woman plucking a chicken was pleading. *"Little Attila has poison ivy. And young Tamerlane's big rockball game is Saturday. You're their daddy. They need you. Can't conquering Europe wait?"*

Maya giggled. "I guess she really can't live without soap operas—even if they're Mongolian soap operas."

Ben went up and tapped Sarah on the shoulder. Unfortunately, it was during the commercial break for Golden Horde Camel Chow. The second

59

Sarah saw the two youngsters, she screamed at the top of her lungs.

Sarah's scream was unlike anything Ben and Maya had ever heard before. It was so high-pitched that dogs all over Irkutsk began howling. As it climbed higher and higher, Maya and Ben covered their ears. Then, all at once, the window beside Sarah's table shattered. Before Ben and Maya knew it, Sarah had jumped out the window. The two ACME aces sprang out onto the platform after her.

"Oh, no," cried Maya. "We'll never catch her—look!"

Ben saw that Sarah had on a pair of in-line skates. She was already fifty yards up the platform, heading toward the front of the train.

Maya and Ben took off after her. But just then the train started moving.

"Forget it, Ben," Maya shouted. "We've got to get back on." They dashed for the door and leaped aboard the train at the last possible moment.

Disappointed, they trudged back to their compartment. As they entered the dining car, though, Ben stopped short. "I don't believe it," he said. There was Sarah Nade, sitting at her table again, staring glassy-eyed at her TV.

"She must have jumped on at the front of the train," said Maya.

Ben and Maya positioned themselves on both sides of Sarah's chair. "No more funny stuff, Nade," Ben said. He flicked off the TV set.

"Give it a rest, flatfoot," Sarah said. "Let me watch my program."

"Why did you run from us?" Maya asked.

"Get real," she replied. "You're ACME, I'm V.I.L.E. Fleeing comes naturally."

"Why didn't you keep on going?"

"And miss my program? No way!" Sarah's eyes started twitching. "Can I please have my TV back now?"

"Not yet," Maya said. "We need to talk to you about a robbery."

"What robbery?"

"King Tut's mummy," Maya said.

Sarah switched the set back on. "I haven't pulled a job in months."

Ben snatched the television off the table. "No talk, no TV."

Sarah was panic-stricken. "No fair. I gotta catch the end of *For Love of Genghis*."

"Then talk," Ben said.

Sarah wilted. "Okay, what do you want to know?"

"What were you doing in Egypt?" Maya demanded.

"I won a contest—'The Time of Your Life Vacation Sweepstakes,'" Sarah said. "First prize was a free trip to Egypt, Russia, and Mongolia. I never won anything legitimately in my life. So I had to go."

Sarah pulled out the notification letter and showed it to them. It looked authentic.

"Did you steal the key to an ACME security crate?" Ben asked.

"Who—*moi*? The only key I know about is C-sharp," she said. "I was skin-diving in the Nile the whole time I was there. You can check on it."

"We will," Ben said. "Meanwhile, you mind if we hold on to this?" he asked, indicating the sweepstakes letter.

"No—as long as you give back my TV."

Ben returned the set. "Where are your V.I.L.E. buddies?"

Sarah smirked. "Gone. They got off at Irkutsk while you were chasing me. And don't ask me where they were going, because I won't tell—*even if you take away my TV.*"

Ben and Maya tried to pump Sarah for more details, but it was no use. With her eyes glued to the TV, she wouldn't talk. Finally, they had to give up. There just wasn't enough evidence to swear out a warrant.

They headed back to their compartment, feeling dejected. Halfway there, Ben stooped to pick something up from the floor. "Hey, what's this?" he said.

It was a postcard. On one side was a picture of hundreds of half-buried red-clay soldiers. On the other, a message that had obviously not been completed:

MY COLLEAGUES IN CRIME:
EVERYTHING GOES SMOOTHLY. NEXT STOP—THE EMPEROR'S SOLDIERS. MAY NEED BIG TRUCK TO MOVE MY TREASU

"I've got a hunch," Ben said, "that this postcard is gonna lead us to King Tut."

6
Xian, Shaanxi Province, China

Jersey was gone! The door to his compartment was open. His bags weren't under his bunk. And a note was pinned to his pillow.

DEAR KIDS:
COULDN'T WAIT. SAW OTHER SUSPECTS ESCAPING. WILL TRACK THEM DOWN MYSELF. SPEAK TO YOU SOON.—JERSEY

Ben stared at the note in disbelief. "How could he leave without us? I thought we were a team— like the Three Musketeers."

"Guess not," Maya said, equally astonished.

Ben's shoulders drooped.

"Hey, c'mon," Maya said, putting a hand on his shoulder. "Since when did this become Jersey's case, anyway? We're the ones The Chief chose—not him. Have we ever needed a third Musketeer before?"

"No, I guess not," Ben said.

"Okay, let's see that postcard again. Maybe we can figure out where Carmen's gang was going in such a rush."

Ben pulled out the postcard. "I've got an idea," he said. "What if I scan the picture and the message into the Sender? Then we can search the database for similar images and words. Maybe we can find a match."

"Good thinking," Maya said. "It's worth a try."

The two friends moved to a small table by the window, and Ben hunched over the Sender keyboard. Maya noticed his spirits perking up with each keystroke.

Minutes later the Sender made a loud *ding!*

"I got tons of matches for *emperor*," Ben said. "You wanna hear them?"

"Read away."

"Okay, let's see," he said. "I've got 'Emperor Napoleon . . . emperor penguin . . . Emperor Waltz . . . Emperors—Chinese . . . Holy Roman

65

Emperor . . .' " He glanced down the list and shook his head. "Rats!" he said. "No direct matches for *emperor's soldiers.*"

"Wait a minute," Maya said. "Run the next to last one by me again."

"You mean 'Emperors—Chinese'?"

"Yeah, that's the one," Maya said. Her eyes lit up, and she bit her bottom lip.

Ben knew that expression well. It meant Maya's wonderful brain had made some connection that even the Sender had missed.

"Sound familiar?" he asked her.

"Sort of. We're on the Mongolian border, right? Well, what's the country just south of Mongolia?"

"Beats me," Ben said. "Hoboken?"

Maya rolled her eyes. "No, doofus, it's China. There were emperors in China for two thousand years. Maybe those red-clay soldiers have something to do with a Chinese emperor." She gestured toward the Sender. "See if you can find anything on Chinese emperors *and* red-clay soldiers."

Ben typed in the commands. In an instant a match flashed on the screen.

QIN SHIHUANGDI: FIRST CHINESE EMPEROR.
RULED AROUND 200 B.C. UNIFIED CHINA. BUILT

GREAT WALL. BURIED WITH ARMY OF RED-CLAY
WARRIORS TO PROTECT HIM AFTER DEATH. SEE
DISPLAY IN MUSEUM IN CITY OF XIAN IN
SHAANXI PROVINCE.

"Call Yul," Maya said. "We need travel arrangements for China."

"Hold on," Ben said. "How can I tell him where we're going when I can't even pronounce it?"

"Just spell it out," she said with a laugh. "And Ben," she added, "tell him this time absolutely, positively no hot-air balloons."

"How old is this thing, anyway?" Ben asked the pilot as the three-seater biplane bumped around in the air above the Mongolian mountains.

The pilot pointed proudly to a tiny plaque by the controls, which read: MADE IN THE USA BY THE WRIGHT BROTHERS. GENUINE BALSA-WOOD FRAME.

"Why did I even ask?" Ben gulped.

As they flew over the mountains, Maya called out the identifying landmarks below.

"That's the Gobi Desert, Ben," she said. "We're almost in China."

"Before we get there," said Ben, "I want to know how to say some of this stuff." He punched

Xian, the name of the city they were heading for, into the Sender.

SHEE-ON, said the Sender.

"That's not so hard," said Maya.

Next, Ben tried Qin Shihuangdi.

CHIN SHUR-HWONG-DEE, replied the Sender.

Maya tried the name. "This stuff is easy if you can deal with the spelling," she said.

Soon they were flying over Chinese villages in the Yellow River valley. Then came a truly breathtaking sight.

"What's that ridge up ahead?" Ben asked above the sputter of the engine. "It seems to go on forever."

"That's no ridge," Maya explained. "That's the Great Wall of China. It's about four thousand miles long. So big, you can even see it from outer space!"

"Awesome!" said Ben.

An hour later the plane touched down in Xian. Using the Sender's translator function, Maya and Ben were able to explain to a taxicab driver where they wanted to go. He took them to a huge marble building on the outskirts of town.

"This is Qin Shihuangdi's Museum of the Warriors and Horses," the cabdriver said in Chinese.

The Sender quickly translated his words into English text.

"Thank you," Ben replied, and two Chinese characters appeared on the screen. Ben pointed to them and asked, "How do you say that?"

謝 謝

"*Shyeh-shyeh,*" the man responded.

"Then *shyeh-shyeh* a lot," Ben said.

The cabdriver gave him a big smile.

Outside the museum door there was a line of schoolgirls in pretty yellow dresses. Maya saw that one girl was giggling and pointing to something on a nearby path. It was a trail of colorful jelly beans that led around back of the building.

"Hmm . . ." said Maya. "Junk food."

Ben looked at her. "Are you thinking what I'm thinking?"

"I'm thinking somebody with a sweet tooth has been by here."

"Me too," Ben said. "Maybe it was Jersey—or one of Carmen's henchpeople?"

"Well, what are we waiting for?" Maya said.

The two ACME sleuths followed the trail of candy. It led toward a second building as big as

an aircraft hangar. Ben and Maya entered cautiously. Inside were rows of long trenches dug into the ground. The trenches were about five feet deep and six feet wide, and they were filled with life-size statues of red-clay soldiers. The figures looked as if they'd somehow been frozen in time as they were marching, four abreast, off to battle.

"Gosh, there are hundreds—maybe thousands—of them!" Ben exclaimed.

"And there's our jelly-bean litterbug," Maya said, pointing to a woman standing beside a trench and arguing with a man in a museum uniform. She was frumpily dressed and had frizzy black hair. She wore thick-rimmed glasses and a cheap necklace made of elbow macaroni and rhinestones. As she gestured wildly at the befuddled man, an occasional jelly bean would drop out of a hole in her handbag.

Ben glanced at the ACME mug shots. "It's Bessie Mae Mucho," he said in a low voice. "According to her dossier, she's a scientific genius. Lives on junk food. Drives a pink Cadillac convertible. Spends her free time skin-diving."

"And maybe stealing mummies," Maya added.

Maya was debating whether they should try to take Bessie by surprise, when the V.I.L.E. gang member caught sight of them and called out, "Yoo-hoo, kiddies! Would you please come over here?"

"Er—sure thing," Maya yelled back, a little unnerved.

"At least she's not running away," Ben said.

The two ACME agents made their way over to the spot where Bessie and the museum official were squabbling.

Ben and Maya identified themselves as ACME detectives. "We're investigating the recent theft of King Tut's mummy," Ben said.

"How very nice for you," Bessie said. "Do you speak Chinese?"

Again Ben and Maya were taken aback by Bessie's totally casual attitude.

"Uh, no, sorry," replied Ben.

"Oh, dear. Well, *he*," she said, her voice dripping with scorn, "doesn't speak any English."

Maya was amazed at how dumb a genius could be. "Hello?" she said. "This is China, not America."

"I know that," Bessie snapped. "But it's utterly impossible that he doesn't understand about my prize."

"What prize?" Ben asked.

"My clay soldier," Bessie replied. "I won it in a travel sweepstakes."

"In a *what*?" Ben asked, remembering the story Sarah had told them.

"I said a travel sweepstakes," Bessie replied with annoyance. "I won first prize in the 'Time of Your Life Vacation Sweepstakes.'" She fished a letter out of her handbag, and a half-dozen more jelly beans scattered on the ground. "It says right here, and I quote: 'First prize is an all-expenses paid trip to Egypt, Russia, Mongolia, and China. While in China, you will get to select—and take home—one of the rare clay soldiers from the Qin Shihuangdi Museum in Xian.'

"Well, I want my prize," Bessie continued. "But this man doesn't seem to know anything about it." A tear slid down her cheek. "You see, it's my birthday in two weeks. Nobody ever gives me anything on my birthday. So I wanted to gift wrap the statue and send it home so I could surprise myself."

Ben showed Bessie the postcard he'd found on the train. "Did you write this?" he asked.

The V.I.L.E. operative's eyes became watery again. "Yes, to my dearest dastardly friends in our gang. But that was before I arrived here to claim my prize. I even arranged for a truck to come pick the statue up for me." She choked up and couldn't continue.

"Here," Maya said, handing Bessie a tissue to dry her tears.

Then Ben used the Sender to explain to the perplexed Chinese official what was going on. The man apologized profusely, but informed Bessie that the museum had a strict policy against giving away clay soldiers to criminals. He also said that he'd never heard of the sweepstakes.

Bessie was so heartbroken, Maya almost didn't want to interrogate her. But she knew that she had to perform her duty.

"I've got to ask you where you were in Cairo when the mummy key was stolen."

"I have an airtight alibi," Bessie replied with a tearful sniff. "I was in jail."

"In jail?" Ben and Maya exclaimed in unison.

"That's right—in the slammer. Right after I left for Cairo, I was arrested by a meter maid from the International Parking Violations Bureau. She said I had $492,677 in unpaid tickets. I thought it was only $352,103." She began to bawl uncontrollably. "Some dream vacation this has been! I didn't even get to *see* Cairo!"

"Listen, Bessie," Ben said. "We know someone in your organization stole King Tut. You can make things easier on yourself if you tell us where

Yul B. Sorry, Bjorn Toulouse, Dazzle Annie Nonker, and Lady Agatha Wayland are right now."

"Oh, go away," Bessie sobbed. "I've got to think of something else to surprise me for my birthday."

The museum guard took pity on Bessie and gave her a pretty glass paperweight with a plastic soldier inside. Maya and Ben left her sniffling softly beside the trench.

"I think it's time that we found out a little bit more about the 'Time of Your Life Sweepstakes,'" Maya said. "Something definitely smells fishy here."

Good! Nobody saw me on that train or lurking behind that clay soldier in Xian. I've got to admit, though, that those two ACME gumshoes, Maya and Ben, make an excellent pair. Worthy opponents in every way. How strange that they're actually helping me in this case. Thanks to them, Sarah, Fast Eddie, and Bessie are now in the clear. Too bad these kids aren't on my side.

I never realized before what a sensitive person Bessie is. I know she'll love the surprise party I've planned for her birthday. And I'm sure she'll love my gift—a reproduction of that statue she wanted. Which member of my gang would dare play such a cruel trick on her? Bjorn? Dazzle Annie? Yul? Lady Agatha? I must get to the bottom of this before anyone else is hurt!

7
Xian, Shaanxi Province, China

Two hours later, Ben and Maya were sitting in a Chinese restaurant. Maya was chasing a fried dumpling around her plate with a pair of chopsticks. Ben had just tapped into CrimeNet and discovered that ACME had no record anywhere of a "Time of Your Life Vacation Sweepstakes." They were both feeling extremely discouraged.

Suddenly Maya poked Ben's hand softly with a chopstick. "Don't turn around," she whispered. "Somebody's watching us."

Ben tilted the Sender screen so that it caught the light at an angle and became glassy, like a mirror. In the reflection he saw an elderly Chinese man peeking at them over his newspaper. The man finished his tea and rose from the table.

"Uh-oh," Ben said. "He's coming over here."

"Just act natural," Maya cautioned.

The man, who had long white hair and a pointy goatee, came up beside Ben.

"Hao Didu," he said.

Ben glanced at the Sender for a translation, but none appeared.

"Hao Didu," the man repeated in a slightly louder voice.

"Er—howdy do to you, too," Ben replied, for lack of anything better to say.

"No—Hao Didu," the man said, extending his hand. "That's my name. You can call me Mr. Hao."

Maya's eyes widened in surprise. "You speak perfect English, Mr. Hao," she said.

"And why not?" the elderly man replied with a grin. "I'm American, just like you. May I join you? I believe I have some information you may find useful."

"Please—be our guest," Ben said.

Mr. Hao pulled over a chair and sat down. "You probably don't know me," he began, "but I'm a former ACME agent. A Hall of Famer, I'm proud to say. Retired years ago. Been traveling round the world, visiting every country in alphabetical order.

I'm already up to C, as you can see."

"Neat," Maya said as her dumpling slipped out of her chopsticks for the third time.

"Yeah, I'd like to do that too when I hang up my badge," Ben said.

Mr. Hao poured himself some tea. "Well, here's the thing. I couldn't sleep last night. So I went down to the local video store to rent a movie. Since I speak Chinese, I thought it would be a hoot to watch the dubbed version of *Star Wars*. But when I got there, the owner was in a total state."

"You mean upset?" Maya inquired.

"Incredibly," Mr. Hao said. "It seems somebody had rented a video and paid with a phony credit card."

In frustration, Maya speared the pesky dumpling with a chopstick. "I don't get it, though. What's this have to do with us?"

"Well," said Mr. Hao, "the shop owner showed me the credit card slip, and guess what? It was a V.I.L.E. Gold Card."

Ben whistled softly. "So it was somebody from Carmen's organization."

"Right," Mr. Hao said.

"Did the owner give you a description of the person?" Maya asked.

Mr. Hao shook his head. "He didn't take the order. His daughter did. And she's not available. She's competing in a kung-fu tournament in another city."

"Rats!" Ben said.

"All's not lost, though," Mr. Hao continued. "We know the name of the video—*Serving on Grass Like a Pro*. And the daughter, who speaks a little English, managed to jot down two strange things the customer said."

Ben's fingers were poised over the Sender keyboard. "Okay, let me have them."

"Well, the first was 'I'm going to look for mobs of joeys.' And the second was something about 'waltzing Matilda.'"

"Nothing more?" Ben asked.

"Sorry, that's it."

"Thanks."

Mr. Hao then politely excused himself. He said he had to hurry to catch the next plane to Colombia.

Maya and Ben pushed their meals aside and began to work on the clues. Ben used the Sender to call up dossiers on the suspects.

"Let's see if they have anything in common," he said. "Maybe that'll help us in some way."

BJORN TOULOUSE. BLOND HAIR, BLUE EYES. TALENTED COUNTERFEITER, HAS A PINK ROSE TATTOO. HOBBY: TENNIS. FOOD: JUNK FOOD. VEHICLE: LIMOUSINE.

YUL B. SORRY. BLACK HAIR, GRAY EYES. SCAR ON LEFT CHEEK. HOBBY: TENNIS. FOOD: JUNK FOOD. VEHICLE: MOTORCYCLE.

DAZZLE ANNIE NONKER. BLOND HAIR, BLUE EYES. HAS A TATTOO, HEALTH-FOOD ADVOCATE. HOBBY: TENNIS. FOOD: SEAFOOD. VEHICLE: LIMOUSINE.

LADY AGATHA WAYLAND. RED HAIR, GREEN EYES. LOVES JEWELRY. HOBBY: TENNIS. FOOD: MEXICAN. VEHICLE: CONVERTIBLE.

CARMEN SANDIEGO. BROWN HAIR, BROWN EYES. FORME ACME DETECTIVE, DRESSES IN RED CLOTHING. HOBBY: TENNIS. FOOD: SEAFOOD. VEHICLE: CONVERTIBLE.

SARAH NADE. BLOND HAIR, GRAY EYES. TV JUNKIE, VERY HIGH-PITCHED VOICE. HOBBY: SKIN-DIVING. FOOD: CHINESE. VEHICLE: LIMOUSINE.

Bjorn Toulouse

Lady Agatha

Sarah Nade

Yul B. Sorry

Carmen Sandiego

Duzzle Annie

Maya examined the dossiers carefully. "Well, first we can rule out Sarah—we have verification on her story. She was skin-diving the whole time she was in Cairo. As for the rest, no more than two of them have the same characteristics or interests—except in one area."

"Oh, yeah?" said Ben. "Which?

"They all like tennis."

Ben thought for a moment. "Wait a minute!" he cried. "That video the customer rented—what was the title again?"

"Serving on Grass Like a Pro," Maya said. "Sounds like a guide to cooking outdoors."

"Could be," Ben said. "But it might also have something to do with tennis. Don't you have to serve the ball to start a game in tennis?"

"You're right!" exclaimed Maya. "And you know what?"

"What?"

"There's a country south of here where they still play a lot of tennis on grass. They call it lawn tennis."

"Don't tell me," Ben said, making a dumb face—*"South* Hoboken?"

Maya gave him a poke in the ribs. "No, wise

guy. The place they call the 'land down under,' Australia."

Ben seemed unconvinced. "But what about the other clues? Mobs of joeys? Waltzing Matilda? They don't make sense."

"Why don't you search for *mob* and *joey* on the Sender," Maya suggested. "See what you get."

Ben typed in the commands, pressed ENTER, and waited.

"Bingo!" he shouted a few minutes later. "According to the *Mostly Reliable Dictionary of Silly-Sounding Words and Phrases*, 'joey' is the Australian nickname for a kangaroo. And—get this!—a whole bunch of kangaroos is called a mob."

"Way to go, Ben!" Maya cried. "Now try the last clue—waltzing Matilda. Is there anything on that?"

Once again Ben's fingers flew over the keyboard. His face registered delight at the results. "We're on a roll. It says here that 'Waltzing Matilda' is a famous Australian song. It's sort of like the unofficial national anthem."

"Yes!" said Maya, exchanging high fives with Ben. "Our suspect's going to Australia. But where? It's almost as big as the U.S. In fact, it's a whole continent by itself."

Ben looked up at Maya. "Maybe I should search for a match for—"

Maya gripped Ben's shoulder. "Say that again."

"I said, maybe I should check for a match—"

"That's it, Ben! You're a genius."

"Huh? What did I say?"

"The magic word—*match*, as in tennis match. Quick, dial up the Internet. Let's see if there are any lawn-tennis matches going on in Australia."

The Sender scanned the Internet and retrieved an article from the *Outback Daily News*. It read:

> Outsiders often say Australia is like no place on earth. We've got red deserts that look like the surface of Mars. We've got plants and animals that exist nowhere else: namely, our gum trees and bush bananas, our koalas and platypuses, and our kangaroos, dingoes, and wombats. Now we've got something even odder to talk about. The International Association of Professional Criminals has decided to hold its annual lawn-tennis championship in our own backyard. The first match in the Criminals' Outback Open begins in Alice Springs, day after tomorrow. . . .

"Oh, good. It's not too late," Ben said, checking another Internet site.

"Too late for what?" asked Maya.

"To get tickets for the matches," Ben replied. He tapped some buttons, then clicked on an icon on the screen. "There," he said. "I've reserved two seats for us at center court, the best in the house."

Ben dialed up Yul on the Sender, expecting the Ruler of All Travel to send them a kite or something. But Yul seemed to be in an excellent mood. "I'm going to give you guys a break," he said. "You've suffered enough."

Yul proceeded to book two flights each for Maya and Ben. The first plane, a comfy jetliner, took them nonstop from Xian to the city of Darwin on the northern coast of Australia. The second, a cargo plane full of mooing cows, deposited them at the airport in Alice Springs, a town situated almost at the dead center of the continent.

Ben gave a shiver as they got off the plane. "Brrr," he said. "Talk about weird weather. This has got to be the coldest day in July on record. It's fr-fr-freezing." He brushed a few strands of hay from his sweatshirt and pulled a light jacket out of his knapsack.

"There's nothing weird about it," Maya explained, putting on her heavy wool sweater.

"Australia's in the southern hemisphere. When we're in summer, they're in winter."

"I n-n-never believed that stuff when I read it in school," Ben said, his teeth chattering. "B-b-but now I do."

Inside the terminal, Ben left Maya to go and buy hot chocolate for both of them. In a moment, the Sender videophone in Maya's pocket began bleeping madly.

It was The Chief, and she looked awfully worried.

"Sorry to bother you, gumshoe," she said to Maya. "But the Egyptians have been bugging me day and night. I need to know if you've made any progress on the Tut case."

Maya took a deep breath. "Well, there's good news and bad news, and then there's some odd news."

The Chief scowled. "Okay, give it to me straight."

Maya measured her words carefully. "The good news is that we've narrowed down our suspect list to five people—including Carmen. We also have reason to believe that the mummy thief is here in Australia."

"Excellent," The Chief said. "Any leads on the whereabouts of Tut?"

Maya shook her head.

"Guess that was too much to expect," The Chief said, looking disappointed. "And your bad news?"

"We still don't have enough information to swear out a warrant."

"You've got all the dossiers, don't you?" The Chief asked anxiously.

"Sure," Maya replied. "But we don't have much hard evidence linking any of them to the crime scene."

"I'm aware of that," The Chief said. "And I'm working to get you some. Right now our top scientists are going over every inch of Tut's crate with a microscope. They found some unusual smudge marks on the inside. I'll fax you the report as soon as it's ready."

"Great," said Maya.

"What about your *odd* news?"

Maya wasn't certain how to put this. "Well, Chief . . . um . . . it looks like Jersey's gone."

"What do you mean, *gone*?"

"Well, it seems he's gone after the thief himself."

"Oh?" The Chief said, raising her eyebrows.

Now came Maya's big question. "Chief, did you give him permission to do that?"

"Certainly not! I told him he should help you, not replace you."

Maya felt relieved. "Chief, could you do me a favor?" she said. "When you fax me, could you also send me whatever data we've got on Jersey? Maybe it'll help us find him."

"You got it, gumshoe!" The Chief said. "Anything to keep some fool amateur from botching this case. He may be an expert archaeologist, or whatever he is, but he's no detective."

By the time Ben returned from the snack bar, The Chief had signed off. Maya filled him in on the details. And as they warmed themselves up with sips of hot chocolate, they both silently wondered what the report from ACME's CrimeLabs would reveal.

8
The Outback, Northern Territory, Australia

The Criminals' Outback Open wasn't actually being held *in* Alice Springs. To get to the tournament, Maya and Ben had to take an old rickety bus about a hundred miles due west, deep into the Australian bush country. The land was flat and dry and covered with fine reddish sand. Occasionally they could see mobs of kangaroos hopping along the roadside.

It was a horrible trip. The bus had no roof and no heat. As it bumped along, dust from the road blew in and carpeted the seats. By the time Maya and Ben arrived at the tournament, they were freezing and sneezing.

Luckily the matches were not taking place

outdoors. They were being played in a heated indoor stadium nestled at the foot of a mountain.

When they got inside, Ben glanced at the scoreboard. The fourth match of the day was about to begin on center court. It pitted Dazzle Annie Nonker against Slim Chantz, the infamous "Cat Burglar of Calcutta." As Ben and Maya took their seats, though, nobody was hitting the ball. Dazzle Annie, dressed in a sporty white outfit with prison bars running across the top, was standing beside the referee's chair with her hands on her hips. She appeared extremely upset. Her opponent didn't look too happy either. He was facing the stands and shaking his fist angrily at the crowd.

The referee got on the squealing loudspeaker. "Okay, mates," he said. "Who's the wise guy? Who stole the lawn?"

Maya gaped at the tennis court. "Jeepers, Ben," she said. "He's right. There's no grass on the court. Somebody must have swiped it."

Ben gazed around the stands. No sign of the lawn anywhere. But he did spot at least three people trying to pickpocket one another. "This crowd's a real bad bunch," he said. "Better watch your wallet."

Maya and Ben gripped their knapsacks tighter.

The loudspeaker squealed again. "Attention! Attention!" the referee said. "Let me remind everyone that this is a *lawn*-tennis championship. We cannot play without the gra—"

The referee broke off as Dazzle Annie whispered something in his ear.

"I have just been informed by Ms. Nonker," he said, "that the net and the tennis balls are also missing. Will the person who stole these things please stand up?"

No one moved.

"Come on," the referee said. "You know who you are. Just give the stuff back. You won't be punished."

A rumble filled the stadium.

"Oh my gosh," Maya exclaimed as everyone in the crowd stood up except for her and Ben.

The referee was so shocked, he didn't know what to say. For a full minute, he buried his head in his hands. When he looked up, his microphone was gone.

He cupped his hands to his mouth and shouted, *"That's it! This tournament is over. Go home—all of you!"*

Just like that, the Criminals' Outback Open had opened and closed.

Maya and Ben sprinted down to the clubhouse to question Dazzle Annie before she packed her rackets and left.

They found her outside the locker room, parked on a wooden bench, munching something green. "Want some?" she asked. "I've got lots more."

The two sleuths sat down beside her.

"What is it?" Ben asked suspiciously.

"Part of the lawn," she said with a devilish smile. "I stole some too. You'd like it. It's full of vitamins."

"Uh—no thanks," Ben said. "I'll take a pass on that."

"Do you know who we are?" Maya inquired.

Dazzle Annie appeared amused by the question. "Sure," she said. "Do you think you're the only ones with dossiers? Carmen's got a computer file on every ACME gumshoe in the world."

Dazzle Annie reached into a canvas bag under the bench. It was bulging with small bottles of vitamins, herbs, spices, and seasonings. "You can never be too healthy," she said, sprinkling a pinch of sea salt on her grass.

Ben gave a loud sneeze. After he wiped his nose, he brought up the Tut heist and observed her reactions. If Dazzle Annie knew anything, she wasn't letting on.

"This is a serious offense," he said. "You'll do a lot of time if you're guilty."

"But I'm innocent as a lamb," she replied, batting her gorgeous blue eyes.

"Come off it, Annie," Ben said, getting tough. "We know you were in Cairo and St. Petersburg. Then you rode the rails to Irkutsk, jumped train, and split to China. Now you've hightailed it here to the outback. Why?"

Dazzle Annie mixed some wheat germ in with her salad. "Why not? I'm traveling around the world—"

"I know, I know," Ben interjected. "I'll bet you won first prize in the 'Time of Your Life Vacation Sweepstakes.' "

"What are you talking about?" Dazzle Annie said. "I'm participating in the Yogurt Caravan."

"The *what*?" Maya exclaimed.

"I guess you guys don't do your homework too well," Dazzle Annie replied. "I own a yogurt bar, Chez Acidophilus. And a month ago I got a simply precious newsletter in the mail. It listed the top ten yogurt bars in the world and the dates that they held their annual yogurt-tasting festivals." She reached into her bag and pulled out the newsletter and a small gift-wrapped package. The wrapping was the same red-and-gold paper as that on the *matryushka* doll, all the way back in Russia!

"I got this box of yogurt samples along with the newsletter," Dazzle Annie said. "I tried a few and they were heavenly. I knew I just *had* to attend these yogurt-tasting events."

Ben sneezed again.

"Bless you," Dazzle Annie said, handing the yogurt samples to Ben. "You can have the rest of these, if you'd like. Yogurt is very good for you. It's full of vitamin Q and polymolybdenum—clears up sneezing fits in a jiffy."

"Thanks," Ben said, accepting the package. "Do you mind if I look at the newsletter, too?"

"Not at all," said Dazzle Annie. "You can have it. I've made my travel plans already. And I always try to make new yogurt fans."

"Two more questions before we let you go, Annie," Maya said. "Where were you when the key to Tut's crate was stolen?"

"Why, I was dining with the Egyptian Minister for Fermented Milk Products. He's got a darling camel-yogurt bar in Alexandria—one of the top ten."

"You were in Alexandria?" Maya said. "That's way north of Cairo."

Dazzle Annie rolled her eyes. "Well, last time I checked it was."

Maya ignored the sarcasm. "Where are your buddies Yul B. Sorry, Bjorn Toulouse, and Lady Agatha Wayland?"

"You know I can't tell you," Dazzle Annie replied. "But I can say this. They played in the first three tennis matches this morning—before that terrible incident with the lawn." She took another bite of grass. "Unfortunately, they all lost and left."

"To where?"

"Uh-uh-uh," Dazzle Annie said, wagging her finger naughtily at Maya. "My lips are sealed."

As Maya and Ben headed for the exit, Ben sneezed violently.

"Remember to take that yogurt," Dazzle Annie yelled. "Get that polymolybdenum working for you."

Outside the stadium, the two ACME sleuths paused by a rock painted with colorful dots, circles, and lines. A man in a down jacket was sitting on

97

top of the rock with paints in hand. He was an aborigine, one of the native Australians whose ancestors had lived on the continent before the English came.

"Like it, mates?" the man said to Maya and Ben.

"It's very nice," Maya replied.

"Americans, huh? I can tell by your accent."

Maya nodded and pointed at the drawing. "What is it?"

"It's a picture of a big lizard we have here called a perentie," he said.

Ben leaned his head to one side, but couldn't find the lizard among all those squiggles and dots. "How long did it take you to do it?" he asked.

"Two days."

Ben shivered. "You mean, you've been out here in the cold for two days?"

"More or less. I don't mind. I'm used to it."

Maya had an idea. She pulled out the mug shots of the remaining three suspects. "Have you seen any of these people?" she asked.

"Hard to say, mate. When people come out of the stadium there, they're all bundled up. But I did hear something strange this morning."

"What?" Ben asked.

"Well, while I was painting the other side of this rock, I heard somebody on this side say something like 'I'm going to cross the phosphorus and see the top cabby.'"

"Was it a man or a woman?" asked Ben.

"It wasn't a deep voice," the aborigine said. "So I couldn't say for sure."

"Thanks for your help," Ben said.

"Want to see my painting on the other side? It's in a different style."

Ben and Maya said yes, and circled around the rock.

"I can't believe it!" exclaimed Maya.

"Pretty good, huh?" the aborigine said.

"Amazing," Ben said with a whistle.

There, on the face of the rock, was a totally realistic painting of the tennis stadium, complete with all the people coming and going outside. In the lower right-hand corner of the painting was a striking brown-haired woman dressed in a classy red hat and red trenchcoat.

"Looks like Carmen's been here too!" said Maya.

9
Istanbul, Turkey

The painter noticed that Ben and Maya were shaking from the cold.

"Why don't you come by my shack?" he said. "It's not far. And I've got a fire going."

Ben and Maya jumped at the offer. They needed a warm place to go to puzzle out their latest clues.

The man, who told them his name was Gonnwit Deewind, led them up a rocky trail that snaked around the mountain. By the time they arrived at his place, Maya and Ben were sweating from the climb.

Gonnwit Deewind threw a log on the fire. "Hungry, mates?" he asked.

"Starved," confessed Maya.

"Good. I got a great dinner for you. It's buried in a pot outside."

"Buried?" Ben said in alarm.

Gonnwit grinned. "Don't worry," he said. "It's fresh. The earth's a natural freezer, you know."

While their new friend went to fetch dinner, the two ACME sleuths sat down cross-legged by the crackling fire.

Ben activated his Sender. "Okay, let's review what we know."

"Well," began Maya, "we know our suspect said something about *crossing the phosphorus* and *seeing the top cabby*."

"That first part just doesn't make sense," Ben said. "Phosphorus is a mineral. You don't cross a mineral. You cross a street or a bridge."

"Right," Maya said, frowning. "What about the second clue? Maybe Top Cabby is an alias for one of Carmen's henchpeople."

Ben did a quick search of all known V.I.L.E. aliases. "I got Hugh R. *Crabby* and *Tip* A. Kanue," he reported, "but no *Top Cabby*."

"Rats!" Maya muttered.

The door opened and a blast of wind momentarily inflamed the burning logs. Gonnwit Deewind strode in carrying a black iron pot, which he placed directly on the fire. In a few minutes the shack was filled with a delicious aroma.

"Stew's done," Gonnwit called, ladling out two bowls for his young guests.

Ben dug into his meal. "Mmm, this is terrific. What is it?"

"I call it my Two-Meat Surprise," Gonnwit said, beaming proudly. "I make it from wombat and barking lizard."

Ben nearly choked. "Did you say *wombat* and *lizard*?"

Gonnwit nodded. "When you cook 'em just right, they get real tender—like chicken or turkey."

"May I be excused?" Ben said, starting to turn green.

"Hold it, Ben," Maya said. "Gonnwit just said something that might be important."

Ben forced himself to swallow. He tried hard not to think about the lump of lizard traveling down his throat.

When he turned to Maya, she was happily polishing off her last bit of stew. "Er—you were saying?"

Maya's brown eyes sparkled in the firelight. "Not me," she said, "Gonnwit. He said this tastes like *turkey*."

"So?" Ben replied.

"*Turkey,*" Maya repeated. "What do you know about it?"

"It's got a beak and wings and we eat it on Thanksgiving."

"No, not that kind of turkey—Turkey the country!"

"Oh, *that* Turkey," Ben responded, his face blushing from embarrassment. "Isn't it in Asia?"

"Most of it," Maya replied. "But there's also a tiny part of the country in Europe, and the two parts are separated by water."

"So?"

"So, one of the bodies of water is called the Bosphorus. Does that ring a bell?"

"Of course!" Ben exclaimed, snapping his fingers. "Bosphorus sounds like *phosphorus*! Maybe our suspect is going to *cross the Bosphorus.*"

"Exactly."

Ben looked sheepish. "Er—Maya, what's across the Bosphorus, anyway?"

"Well, a lot of places, actually. But I've got a strong hunch our culprit is headed for the city of Istanbul."

"How do you figure that?"

"Elementary, my dear Benjamin," Maya said in

her best Sherlock Holmes voice. "Half of Istanbul is in Asia and half in Europe. On the European side there's a famous palace where the sultans of Turkey used to live. It's a museum now. It's called the Topkapi."

Suddenly Ben got it. "So our suspect needs to *cross the Bosphorus* in order to *see the Topkapi!*"

"Right," Maya said. "And so do we."

While Gonnwit put up some water for tea, Ben and Maya called Yul on the videophone and asked him to book them on an overnight flight to Istanbul. The ACME travel agent took down their exact location, checked his flight program, then furrowed his brow.

"Sorry, kids," he said. "I can't get a plane to you for another two days."

"What?" Maya cried. "We can't afford to lose two days. Who knows where our suspect will be by then."

"I'm sorry," said Yul glumly.

"Don't you have *anything* you can book us on?" Maya pleaded. "Anything at all?"

Yul thought for a while. "There is one possibility," he said. "But it's extremely risky."

"We'll try it," Maya said. "We're desperate."

"I know I shouldn't be doing this," Yul said, shaking his head. "But I guess there's no other choice. Now, listen closely."

Ben and Maya inched closer to the Sender screen.

Yul took a deep breath. "Each of you has an Ultra-Secret Sender 333X, right?"

The two agents nodded.

"Well, that X stands for experimental. And that's because the 333X has got an LDADTR chip inside."

"A what?" Maya asked blankly.

Ben offered to explain. "ACME scientists have been working on the LDADTR for years. It stands for Long-Distance Anthropo-Demolecularizer Transporter and Reverser."

"What's this LDADTR do?" Maya asked.

"In theory," Yul said, "it can transport you anywhere in the world at the press of a button."

"Only *in theory*?" Maya said.

"I'm afraid so," Yul replied gravely. "We've never tested it with humans. Only soup cans. And some of them come through dented—or worse."

"What do you mean, *worse*?" Ben asked.

Yul gazed down at his desk. "We don't know why, but a few cans sort of . . . get lost in the fourth dimension."

The ACME travel agent paused to let this information sink in. "Do you still want to do it?"

Maya and Ben looked at each other. They knew this was their only hope of catching up to their prime suspects and saving ACME from certain economic ruin.

"We'll do it!" they said.

It took Yul half an hour to teach them how to activate the LDADTR function. Before he signed off, he said, "I'll be monitoring the path of your molecules every second. And I want you to know that if anything happens"—he broke off, his voice choked with emotion—"I won't rest until I get you back safely. Good luck, gumshoes. It's been an honor knowing you."

As Yul's face faded from the screen, Maya and Ben found two cups of tea waiting for them. They drank them slowly, as if the cups were their last. Then they bid Gonnwit Deewind a fond farewell and thanked him for his hospitality.

Outside, on the mountain slope, they activated their Senders. Ben programmed the LDADTRs on both devices with the coordinates for Istanbul.

"Sure hope I don't mess this up," said Maya.

"You won't," said Ben.

"Best friends?" said Maya.

"Best friends," said Ben.

"Okay," Maya said. "Here's goes nothing."

Then the two ACME agents pressed ENTER and vanished, with a soft popping sound, into thin air.

Maya felt as if she were traveling on a roller coaster through a dark tunnel. She couldn't see herself or Ben. At the end of the tunnel was a dimly lit figure who seemed to be wearing a beehive-shaped hat. The figure got closer and closer. Then Maya heard another soft popping noise.

Everything suddenly looked normal—at least, normal for wherever it was she'd landed. Maya found herself standing in a narrow cobblestone street lined on both sides with hundreds of small shops and street carts. Mustachioed men and kerchiefed women were selling everything from Oriental rugs and gold jewelry to porcelain vases and shiny leather jackets.

Maya breathed a deep sigh of relief. The Sender had brought her through safely. The whole trip, she guessed, had taken no more than five minutes. She wondered when Ben would be reappearing.

"Welcome to the Covered Bazaar," said a boy's voice from the nearby sidewalk. "You walk as quietly as a cat. I didn't see or hear you coming."

Maya glanced at the boy and realized instantly that this was the figure she'd seen at the end of the tunnel. Only he wasn't wearing a hat at all. He was balancing a huge plate of steaming rolls on his head.

"You speak English?" Maya said.

"A little," the boy replied. "I learn it in school. My name's Kemal."

"And mine's Maya," the ACME sleuth said. "Now, I know this is going to sound crazy, Kemal. But the Covered Bazaar—it's in Istanbul, right?"

Kemal gave her an odd look. "Where else? It is the largest covered bazaar in the world. There are four thousand shops along these streets."

"Right," Maya said. "I knew that. It's just that sometimes you land in weird places and you need to double-check that where you've landed is where you wanted to go."

The boy looked at her blankly. Clearly he hadn't understood a word of what she'd said.

"Uh, sorry, that was too hard," Maya murmured as she searched the passing crowd for signs of Ben. She was starting to get worried. Ben should have materialized by now.

"Kemal," she said. "You haven't seen a boy around here, have you? He's American. Your

109

height. Curly blond hair. Blue eyes."

Kemal shook his head.

Then it occurred to Maya that Ben might have arrived earlier and gone off looking for her. "Is the Topkapi Museum near here?" she asked.

"Yes," Kemal replied. "If you walk ten blocks east, you cannot miss it. It is in a big park, and there is a beautiful fountain outside the gate."

"Thanks, Kemal," Maya said. "You've been a big help."

"Then I am happy," the boy said. "In Turkey, it is a blessing to help a stranger."

Maya ran and made it to the Topkapi in no time. That was quite a feat in itself. The curbs in Istanbul were so high that she had to leap every time to reach the sidewalk.

The Topkapi was an incredible sight. A former palace, it sparkled like a jewel on the tip of Istanbul. It had three huge courtyards and a building called the Harem, where the ruler's many wives lived. It also contained a Muslim holy place, where relics once owned by the prophet Muhammad were kept.

Maya didn't know where to begin looking for Ben—or their three remaining suspects. But she knew that the Topkapi had some of the biggest diamonds in the world. So she made a beeline for the jewel rooms.

It was there that she spotted Lady Agatha Wayland, ogling the famous Spoonmaker diamond.

"You can look, but you can't touch, Lady Agatha," Maya said.

Lady Agatha turned around and gave Maya a withering stare. "Oh, yeah?" she sniffed. "Well, children are meant to be seen, not heard."

"Oh, yeah?" Maya countered. "Well, it's better to be safe than sorry."

Lady Agatha sneered at her. "Oh, yeah?" she said. "Well, she who laughs last laughs loudest."

"Oh, yeah?" Maya shot back. "Well, top *this*— sticks and stones may break my bones, but crime doesn't pay."

"Huh?" said Lady Agatha. "You're not playing fair. That's not a real proverb."

"Well, stealing a world treasure isn't exactly playing cricket either."

"What are you talking about, you little beast?" snipped Lady Agatha. "I wasn't stealing this diamond, I was merely admiring it." She slid her glasses down to the tip of her nose and glared at Maya. "There's no crime in that, is there?"

Maya was trying hard to keep her cool. "I'm

not talking about diamonds, Lady Agatha," she said. "I'm talking about something bigger. I'm talking about—"

At that moment, Maya's Sender began beeping loudly, signaling that a fax was coming through.

"Will you excuse me?" Maya said. "I'll return to our argument in a second."

Lady Agatha tapped her foot angrily. "I'll wait. I wouldn't miss it for the world."

The fax was from The Chief. It was marked TOP SECRET, URGENT, INCREDIBLY HUSH-HUSH. It read:

DEAR GUMSHOES:

AT LAST! OUR FIRST BIG BREAKS!

• ANALYSIS BY ACME LABS REVEALS SMUDGES INSIDE CRATE ARE MADE OF MILK CHOCOLATE AND NOUGAT. OUR THIEF HAS A CRAVING FOR JUNK FOOD.

• ALTHOUGH NO RECORD EXISTS OF "TIME OF YOUR LIFE SWEEPSTAKES" OR "YOGURT CARAVAN," A DATABASE SCAN REVEALS BJORN TOULOUSE AND YUL B. SORRY WERE INVOLVED IN FALSE SWEEPSTAKES SCAMS BEFORE JOINING V.I.L.E.

• STILL CHECKING INFO ON JERSEY. WHEREABOUTS STILL UNKNOWN.

GOOD LUCK,

THE CHIEF

Maya stuffed the fax in her knapsack and pulled out a copy of Ben's suspect list. Then she walked back to Lady Agatha.

"Well?" the V.I.L.E. operative grumbled.

Maya glanced at the chart. "I have only one question for you," she said.

"Yes?"

"If you could choose between two scoops of Rocky Road ice cream in a sugar cone and a meal in the finest restaurant in Paris, which would it be?"

Lady Agatha looked at Maya suspiciously. "Is this some kind of trick?" she said. "I wouldn't choose either. I only like Mexican food."

"Just checking," Maya said. "Now, why don't you just make like an egg and beat it."

After Lady Agatha left, Maya searched the Topkapi from top to bottom for Ben and the other two suspects. They were nowhere to be found. Then came another beep on the Sender. This time it was the videophone.

Maya hated having to deal with the Sender in Ben's absence, but somehow she managed to press the right buttons.

It was Yul. His face was ghost white. "Something awful has happened," he said.

Maya knew instantly. "Ben! It's Ben, isn't it?"

Yul nodded. "We've lost his molecules in the fourth dimension."

"Yul! How could you?" Maya screamed. "You promised to watch out for us!"

"I did. Believe me, I did. But he ran into some dimensional turbulence along his flight path."

"Get him back, Yul!" Maya shouted.

"I will," the travel agent promised. "I've almost got the problem figured out. And when I do, I'll beam his molecules on to Iceland."

"Iceland?" Maya said.

"Reykjavík, to be precise. We just got an E-mail from Jersey. He said our two remaining suspects are headed for Carmen's base there. He'll meet you at the Blue Lagoon. I've booked you on the next jet from Istanbul."

"All right," Maya said. "But when I get there, Ben had better be there too."

10
The Blue Lagoon, Iceland

It happened like magic. As Maya's plane was landing at Keflavík Airport in Iceland, something in the seat next to her went *pop!* She looked and gasped. It was Ben! He'd rematerialized from the fourth dimension.

"See, Maya," Ben said, fussing with his crooked glasses. "I told you there was nothing to worry about. You made it through okay. You handled the Sender like a champ."

Maya threw her arms around him. "Shut up, you big jerk," she said. "I've never been so happy to see somebody's molecules in my entire life."

"Huh?" Ben said, squirming in his seat. "What was *that* for?"

Maya stared straight into his eyes. "Ben, do

115

you have any memory of where you've been?"

"Uh, sure," he said. "I remember riding this roller coaster through a dark tunnel. Then there was a flash of orange light, and suddenly I'm floating around in a sea of dented soup cans. Pretty weird, huh? Next thing I know, I'm back in the tunnel again. Then I hear a *pop!*—and here I am!"

"Okay," Maya said. "You'd better sit back and relax, because I've got a few things to tell you."

By the time the plane had taxied up to its gate at the terminal, Maya had briefed Ben about everything: the mishap with his LDADTR, her encounter with Lady Agatha, and the communications from The Chief and Yul.

"Whew!" Ben said. "Guess I'm lucky to be here at all."

"No, I'm the lucky one," Maya said. "I can't solve this case without the best partner in the world."

Maya and Ben hailed a taxi outside the terminal and asked the driver to take them to the Blue Lagoon.

"What's that?" Ben asked as they pulled out of the airport.

"Well," Maya replied, "I did some homework on the plane right before you popped in."

"By yourself—with the Sender?"

"Uh-huh," Maya said.

"Excellent!"

Maya beamed proudly. "I discovered that the Blue Lagoon is an enormous outdoor swimming pool southwest of Reykjavík, the capital."

"Cool," Ben said.

"No, warm," replied Maya. "Iceland is up by the Arctic Circle. But it's got a lot of volcanoes. So if you dig far enough into the ground you actually hit rock that's so hot it can boil water."

"No fooling?"

"No fooling. But that's not the neatest part. The Icelanders love their country and want to keep it as free of pollution as possible. So they sank pipes deep into the ground to tap all that natural heat. It's called geothermal energy. And they use that energy to make electricity, to heat their homes and schools, and even to melt snow off their streets and sidewalks in winter."

Ben's eyes widened. "You mean, they don't burn oil or gas? They heat their homes with water from—from volcanoes?"

"That's the general idea."

"That's *s-o-o-o* cool—oops, I mean *s-o-o-o* warm," Ben said. "But what's this got to do with the Blue Lagoon?"

"I'm getting to that," Maya said. "We're supposed to meet Jersey at one of Iceland's biggest geothermal stations. It pumps hot water from the earth into Reykjavík. But some of that water is also used to fill this huge swimming pool, called the Blue Lagoon. The pool is always warm—even when it's freezing out."

Ben poked around in his knapsack. "Rats!" he said. "I forgot to bring my swimsuit."

The Blue Lagoon was packed with vacationers. Maya saw children in rubber rafts paddling past gumdrop-shaped rocks covered with white mineral deposits. On the far side of the lagoon stood the silver-colored pipes of the geothermal power station. Steam was pouring into the air from its towering funnels.

While waiting for Jersey, Maya and Ben slipped off their shoes. They sat down by the pool's edge and dangled their feet in the water.

"You hungry?" Maya asked.

"No way," Ben replied.

"Well, I am."

"I'm sure you could get a snack on the other side of the pool."

Maya pouted. "I don't want to get up," she said, kicking the water in a mock temper tantrum. "You get it for me. I'm jet-lagged."

Ben dodged the splashes and grinned. "Oh, yeah? Well, I'm fourth dimension–lagged."

Maya's face brightened. "Got any food in your knapsack?"

"Maybe," Ben said. "Lemme see." He went rooting around in his knapsack. "I have a broken pretzel stick, a bag of red hots, a few breath mints, and—hey!—Dazzle Annie's box of yogurt samples."

"Yes!" shouted Maya. "The boy saves the day again!"

Maya chose a cup of lemon-kiwi-coconut meringue and peeled back the seal.

"Oh, gross!" she exclaimed.

"What's the matter?" Ben asked. "Don't tell me it's got furry green stuff on it."

"No, it's not spoiled," Maya said. "It's got a hair in it."

"It's probably Dazzle Annie's," Ben said. "Throw the cup away and take another."

Maya started to get up, then stopped. "Wait a

minute," she said. "How could it be Annie's? The cup was sealed. Besides, Annie's a blonde. This hair is black." She lifted it out so that Ben could see it.

"Yuck!" Ben said. "You'd think they'd wear hair nets at the yogurt factory."

"Maybe they do," said Maya, thinking out loud. "But maybe the person who filled this cup didn't. And maybe that person is the same person who sent Annie on the Yogurt Caravan."

"And the others on the 'Time of Your Life Vacation Sweepstakes'!" Ben said excitedly.

"Right!" Maya said. "Which means our thief has black hair."

"*May* have black hair," Ben corrected. "We shouldn't jump to conclusions. It could still be from an innocent person."

"I know, I know," Maya said. "But I just have a hunch we're closing in on our culprit."

Just then Maya felt something tugging on her toe. Staring down into the water, she saw a chubby man outfitted in a scuba suit. He surfaced amid a gush of bubbles.

"Jersey?" Maya ventured.

The swimmer removed his face mask. "None other," he said. He raised an arm from the water. "Help me out, will ya?"

Maya shot him a dark look. "I don't know whether to give you a hand or duck you under. You ran out on us in Irkutsk."

"I left you a note, didn't I?"

"And you said you'd contact us, but you didn't," Maya shot back. "What did you think you were doing?"

Jersey struggled out of the water, grunting like a walrus. "What's your problem, anyway?" he said. "You kids should be thankful I took off."

"Thankful?" Maya exclaimed. "I don't know what rules you play by, but Ben and I are gathering evidence for a warrant. For all we know, you could have totally messed things up."

"Me? Mess things up? Never!" Jersey snapped. "Why, I'm two steps away from smoking out Carmen and solving this case. If it weren't for me, both of you would be stuck back in St. Petersburg without a clue."

Ben couldn't believe what he was hearing. "This isn't *your* case, Jersey," he said. "It's *ours.* Maybe I'm blind, but I don't see your ACME badge. Or your assignment letter from The Chief. When you show them to us, we'll let you run this case. In the meantime, Maya and I are the only detectives on this job. And if you don't like it, you'd better take off again—right now!"

Jersey seemed stung by Ben's outburst. "Hey, now, little buddy," he said with a nervous grin. "Take it easy. I didn't mean any offense. We're a team, right?" He extended his hand.

Ben made no move to take it. "No more surprises like Irkutsk?" he said.

"I promise," Jersey swore.

"Who's in charge?" Ben asked.

"Why—you two, of course."

"Okay, then," Ben said, slowly reaching for Jersey's hand. "But you're on probation."

Jersey winced. "Fair enough, little buddy. I don't want to do anything to mess up our case against Carmen."

"Good," Ben said, "because we're closing in on our man. We've narrowed our suspects down to two: Yul B. Sorry and Bjorn Toulouse."

"That's just the guy I was spying on here!" Jersey said.

"Who?" Maya asked.

"Bjorn. He's over there—in the water."

Maya looked to where Jersey was pointing and saw an athletic-looking man with curly blond locks and baby blue eyes riding an inflatable rubber ducky. He was surrounded by a swarm of rubber canoes containing giggling teenage girls in bikinis.

"That's Bjorn, all right," Ben said. "I don't know why, but girls seem to go crazy over him."

"Well, he *is* kind of cute," Maya said, blushing.

"Don't let his looks fool you," Ben warned. "He's the world's most notorious counterfeiter."

"You mean he makes fake money?"

"That's what it says in his dossier."

"What a waste," Maya said. "He's got such adorable curls."

Ben rolled his eyes. "Forget about his curls. He's a suspect. Do you think we should question him here?"

"No, no, no," Jersey cut in. "Let's tail him and see if he leads us to Carmen's secret base in Reykjavík."

Maya and Ben thought that over.

"Okay, we'll do it," Maya said at length. "But we're not entirely sure Bjorn's our man. We think the thief's hair may be black. But if we can eliminate him from our list, that leaves only one suspect—Yul B. Sorry."

And so they waited . . . and waited . . . and waited. Finally, two hours later, a slightly overcooked Bjorn slipped out of the water and hopped into a limousine. Maya, Ben, and Jersey piled into a taxi right behind.

"Gódan daginn," the cabby said.

"Good day to you, too," Jersey replied.

"Tell him to follow that car," Maya instructed.

Jersey muttered a few words in Icelandic, and the cabby nodded his head. *"Já, já,"* he said.

Bjorn's limousine headed up the coast, with Maya and Ben's taxi in close pursuit. They passed black lava fields and small villages with racks of fish hanging outside to dry.

In Reykjavík, Bjorn pulled up to a sport shop and went inside.

"You guys stay here," Maya said. "I'll question him myself. He may react better to a girl."

"Don't let those baby blue eyes snow you," Ben called after her.

Inside the shop, Bjorn was standing by the cash register arguing with the owner. In his hands was what looked like a painting.

"But I need a new tennis racket," Bjorn was saying. "Mine got stolen in Australia."

"I'm terribly sorry," the owner said. "But I cannot accept this as payment."

Maya approached and saw that the painting was

of some kind of Icelandic paper money—a five thousand *krónur* bill.

"This is a work of art," Bjorn said. "It's worth more than the price of a new tennis racket."

"It's just a painting, and not a very good one at that," the store owner said. "Besides, it's illegal to accept counterfeit money."

"Hold it, sir, if you don't mind," Maya said, flashing her ACME badge. "I need to talk to this man."

"Be my guest," the owner said. "But don't ask him to make change."

Maya spent the next few minutes interrogating Bjorn. She quickly learned that Bjorn had won first prize in the "Counterfeiters' Caravan Sweepstakes." He proudly showed her some of the crayon sketches he'd made of Egyptian, Russian, Chinese, and Australian money.

At this point Maya was beginning to have serious doubts that Bjorn had stolen the mummy. But the clincher came when Bjorn revealed that he was appearing on an Egyptian cable TV program—*How to Paint Money on Felt*—at the time Tut vanished. A quick call to Cairo on the Sender confirmed Bjorn's story.

"I guess nobody in V.I.L.E. got to see your

show," Maya said innocently. "They all seem to have been busy at the time."

"Yeah," Bjorn said. "It was the strangest thing. Everybody decided to go on vacation all at once."

"Even your buddy Yul B. Sorry?"

Bjorn nodded sadly. "But it's okay. The cable station in Cairo is going to play a tape of it tomorrow. He'll be able to see it then."

"That's great news!" Maya said, dashing for the door.

"Isn't it?" Bjorn replied.

Now at last I know who was trying to frame me. And where the mummy is. What a surprise! How could I be so blind? I should always trust my instincts on things like this. I'm never wrong. No time to lose! I've got to get back to Cairo. I've got a little surprise in store for the real Tut thief.

11
Cairo, Egypt

Maya, Ben, and Jersey took a jet from Reykjavík to Cairo. They were tuckered out from chasing the Tut thief all over creation. "I'm going to sleep for a while," said Ben, nestling into his tiny airline pillow.

"Me too," said Maya, closing her eyes. "I'm glad we're just about at the end of this case."

When they reached Egypt, they checked into the Cairo Prakturr Hotel. It was a small place, with elaborately carved balconies that overlooked the street.

Maya had just sat down on her bed with the Sender when Ben burst into her room.

"Stop!" he yelled.

"What the—?" Maya exclaimed.

"Don't do it!"

Maya set the Sender down on the coffee table. "Calm down, Ben," she said. "I was just going to call Wanda the Warrant Officer and ask her to draw up a warrant for Yul B. Sorry's arrest."

"Good," Ben gasped. "I caught you in time." He staggered over to a chair and collapsed in it. "I didn't want us to go through that again."

"Go through what? What are you babbling about? Why are you so out of breath?"

Ben waited for his heart to stop racing. "Remember that case we had, when Carmen stole the colors from the Painted Desert?"

"How could I forget?" Maya said.

"Well, remember how we thought we had it all figured out? And we ordered a warrant for Dee Molish's arrest?"

"Boy, do I ever," Maya said, shaking her head. "Dee didn't do it. We nearly got kicked out of ACME for swearing out a false warrant."

"Exactly," Ben said. "And we'd better not do that again."

"What do you mean?" Maya said.

Ben was breathing more easily now. "Well, I don't want to blow this case, because we've been tricked."

"Tricked? By whom?"

"I'm not totally sure yet," Ben said, "but look at these."

He reached into his jacket pockets and pulled out about a dozen yellowing newspaper articles. Then he spread them out like playing cards on the table. CARMEN SANDIEGO STEALS CRADLE OF CIVILIZATION blared one headline. HEEL ON BOOT OF ITALY MISSING! screamed another. LADY IN RED STRIKES AGAIN! ADDS CAPE OF GOOD HOPE TO DAZZLING WARDROBE read a third. Maya cast her eyes over the others. All were stories about Carmen's brilliant capers and ACME's valiant efforts to foil the criminal genius. There were even a few articles about Ben and Maya's exploits.

"Where did you get these?" she asked.

"Jersey's room."

Maya whistled softly. "What were you doing in there?"

"It was totally an accident," Ben said. "I went down to let him know we were finally going to issue a warrant. But when I knocked on his door, nobody answered. So I sort of turned the doorknob and went in."

"*Accidentally*, of course."

130

Ben blushed. "Honest, Maya, I didn't mean to snoop. It's just that I guess I panicked. I thought maybe he'd run off again. I wanted to see if his bags were still there."

"And?"

"They were, including the gym bag in which he said he kept his dirty laundry."

Maya sat up straight. "You're not telling me these clips were in there?"

"Uh-huh," Ben said. "He left the zipper open. I could see the bag was full of them. It was like a portable library of articles—all of them about Carmen and ACME."

"Do you think he was lying to us about the laundry?"

Ben shrugged. "Either that or he moved his dirty socks somewhere else."

"That's so weird," Maya said. "Why would an explorer carry around old articles about Carmen?"

"Beats me," Ben said. "But from the very beginning he seemed to know a lot about V.I.L.E."

"That's true," Maya agreed. "But maybe it's one of his hobbies. I mean, a lot of people are crazy about crime stories and cop shows on TV."

"You're right," Ben said. "But that's not all I

found in Jersey's bag." Ben reached into his pocket again and pulled out what looked like a long, squiggly nail.

"It's the key to the ACME security crate!" exclaimed Maya in surprise.

"Right," said Ben. "And do you remember how he told us he keeps it on his person at all times?"

"That's right, he did!" said Maya. "So why was it in this bag with the clippings?"

"Good question. So now I'm beginning to wonder if it's Jersey's key or the missing third key."

"Omigosh!" Maya cried. "Do you think it's possible Jersey stole it from the Cairo museum?"

"I guess anything's possible in a case like this."

Maya suddenly grew worried. "Ben, you've got to return these things at once. Jersey can't know that we suspect him."

Ben sprang up and ran toward the door.

"No, wait—come back!" Maya called. She rummaged frantically in her knapsack and seized a bottle of purple nail polish. "Give me the key," she said. Hands trembling, she placed a tiny drop of purple fluid on the head of the nail and blew on it. "There, now we can tell the two keys apart. Run—and hurry back, safely."

The call from The Chief came while Ben was out on his urgent mission. Maya was almost too distracted to notice that Aunt Velma was smiling.

"I knew I made the right choice in assigning this case to you and Ben," The Chief said. "You've both got gumshoe instincts and gumshoe noses." She held up a thick computer printout for Maya to see. "There's something fishy about this case. And you smelled it halfway around the world."

Maya tried hard to concentrate. "What's that?" she asked.

"The background report you requested on Jersey Jones."

At the mention of the explorer's name, Maya snapped alert. "Good grief—you mean that huge printout is all about him?"

The Chief nodded, and flipped through the pages. "Just about everything's in here. Expeditions. Safaris. The trip around Antarctica in a kayak. The search for the gold of Genghis Khan. The translation of *Winnie the Pooh* into hieroglyphics."

"Anything a little more useful?" Maya asked.

"You may have noticed I said *just about* everything."

Maya was puzzled. "You mean there's stuff missing?"

"A lot," said The Chief. "Our data on Jersey Jones goes back ten years and then stops cold. We can't even locate his birth certificate."

"I don't get it, Chief. What are you saying—that Jersey doesn't exist?"

"Not exactly. I'm saying the man called Jersey Jones has another identity."

Maya's jaw dropped. "How do you know that for sure?"

The Chief lifted another document. "We took one of Jersey's current pictures and ran it through a computer. The computer was able to morph Jersey's image and show us roughly what Jersey looked like ten years ago." She showed Maya the resulting image. Jersey's face appeared thinner. His hair was longer. And he had no mustache.

"Old Fred, the janitor who's been sweeping the halls here for twenty years, never forgets a face," The Chief said. "And he recognized this one instantly as Daley Bredd."

"Jersey is really named Daley Bredd? Who's that?"

The Chief sighed. "It's a sad story, I'm afraid. Daley Bredd was one of our most promising applicants for gumshoe training school. But we could accept only one new recruit that year, and there was someone else who was far superior in every way."

"Don't tell me—Carmen?"

"You got it."

Suddenly everything was clear to Maya. "So Carmen beat out Daley Bredd for a spot at ACME. And Daley Bredd has been harboring a grudge ever since."

"That's the way I see it, gumshoe."

"Thanks, Chief," Maya said. "You've been an enormous help."

"That's what we're here for," said The Chief.

Suddenly Maya had a brainstorm. "Chief," she said, "I know what we need to do to smoke out our thief. I'm going to need your help. Can you arrange to transport a big tent to the desert by tomorrow?"

"I think it can be arranged," The Chief said, and then paused. "For what it's worth," she added wistfully, "nobody wants to catch Carmen more than I do. But Carmen believes in fair play. And so do I. I won't let anybody frame her. So you go get the goods on Jersey Jones—and then we'll nail him!"

When Ben returned, Maya was overjoyed to learn that he'd managed to slip the clippings and key back into Jersey's gym bag undetected.

"So far, so good," Maya said. Then she sat Ben down and told him about her conversation with The Chief, and about her great brainstorm.

"You're sure you want to do it this way?" Ben asked. "It's totally unconventional, and pretty risky."

"I think it's our only chance of recovering King Tut."

"Okay," Ben said. "I sure hope you know what you're doing."

Maya laughed. "Just think of it this way. We can't go to the mountain. So we're going to make the mountain come to us."

Oh," said Ben, "is *that* what we're doing?"

Maya strapped on her knapsack. "Remember, your job is to write the note. My job is to set the trap." She scurried out the door. "Wish me luck," she called. "I'm off to find the cheese."

The streets of Cairo were teeming with life. Women in long embroidered dresses pressed jasmine and spices on Maya. A small herd of camels rumbled by, led by a youth in a white robe and turban. Maya kept walking, making her way toward the Nile River.

Soon she crossed a bridge guarded by huge lion

statues. Beneath her rushed the dark waters of the Nile, and on it floated a fleet of wooden sailboats.

At last Maya reached her destination, a small stone house off a narrow alley. She knocked on the door, and a tall man with jet-black hair and a scarred left cheek answered. He looked surprised to see Maya.

"May I come in?" Maya said. "I've got a proposition for you."

At about the same time, Jersey returned to his hotel room to find a note slipped under his door.

DEAR JERSEY:

GREAT NEWS! WE'VE LEARNED THAT YUL B. SORRY WILL BE MEETING CARMEN SOMEWHERE OUTSIDE CAIRO. WE'RE GOING TO TAIL HIM THERE AND TRY TO FIND KING TUT. IF WE DO, WE'LL ARREST CARMEN. YUL'S LEAVING BY MOTORCYCLE TOMORROW AT NOON FROM THE TAHRIR BRIDGE. WE'LL TELL YOU ALL ABOUT IT WHEN WE GET BACK.

BEN AND MAYA

The next day Maya and Ben sat on a motor scooter. They watched as Yul B. Sorry revved up his large, fancy motorcycle and took off into the

Egyptian desert. The two ACME agents strapped on their helmets and, with Maya driving, blasted off in the same direction.

Wind whistled through their hair, and sand bit at the exposed parts of their necks and faces.

"We're heading toward Giza," Maya called out to Ben. "That's where the three greatest pyramids of Egypt were built. Look! You can see them from here."

Ben saw the three immense stone wedges rising up from the horizon. "Amazing. Was that where Tut was buried?" he asked.

"Not, not in Giza," shouted Maya. "In the Valley of the Kings, farther south."

Ben heard the roar of a big truck behind them. Someone was honking furiously, wanting to pass. Maya pulled over to the shoulder and stopped as a huge truck hurtled past.

"Crazy driver!" screamed Ben.

"Yeah," said Maya. "Real crazy."

Ben and Maya's scooter was slower than Yul's motorcycle. By the time they arrived at Giza, Yul B. Sorry was already inside a big canvas tent set up in the lengthening shadow of the Great Pyramid

of Cheops. Maya and Ben parked their scooter and approached the entrance cautiously.

Maya put one finger to her lips. "Shhh," she whispered, and softly moved forward.

Ben nodded and tiptoed beside her.

Then, suddenly, a voice boomed out from behind them. *"Stand back! Let an expert take over!"*

Jersey jumped out from behind a palm tree and rushed toward the tent flap. "The game's up, Carmen!" he shouted. "Come on out! You're going to spend the rest of your life behind bars."

"Jersey, what are you doing?" yelled Maya.

"I'm about to make a citizen's arrest of Carmen Sandiego."

"I told you before," Maya said. "We can't arrest her without a warrant. And we can't get a warrant without evidence. We need to find the mummy."

"Um—that's easy enough," Jersey said. "She must have hidden it somewhere nearby." He gestured toward to a large mound of sand a few yards from the tent. "There—that's a likely spot. Dig around there, and I bet you'll find it. Meanwhile I'll go in and arrest Carmen."

"It's a deal," Maya said.

Jersey stormed through the opening in the tent.

"Looking for someone?" Yul B. Sorry said. He was all alone in the tent.

"Where's Carmen?" Jersey said, flabbergasted. "Did she escape?"

"She was never here, Jersey," Maya called from the entrance. "Or should I call you Daley Bredd?"

Jersey Jones's face turned white. "How did you know my name?"

"Creative sleuthing," Maya said.

Ben rushed into the tent, grinning from ear to ear. "They're there!" he cried. "Tut's coffin and mummy are buried in the sand!"

Maya walked over to Yul B. Sorry. "Thanks for your help," she said. "We couldn't have done it without you."

"Don't mention it," Yul said. "I may be a crook, but I don't frame innocent criminals. Besides, Carmen told me you might be stopping by. She said I should cooperate with you."

"She knew all along?" Ben exclaimed.

"I never ask her what she knows or when she knows it," Yul said. "But believe me, that lady knows a lot." Then Yul went over and poked Jersey in the chest. "Listen up, Jersey Schmerzy. Now I want *you* to know something. Carmen is one swell boss—you hear? And if you ever get out of the slammer—which I seriously doubt—I don't want to see you having another one of your bright ideas. 'Cause remember this: Yul B. Sorry doesn't ever forget—*ever*."

Yul picked up his crash helmet and exited the tent. "See you around the next crime scene," he said.

"You've got no reason to hold me," Jersey said to the two junior detectives. "It's pure coincidence the mummy was found here."

"It won't work, Jersey," Ben said. "There are tire tracks in the sand that lead to your truck. You had the mummy all along. Back at the beginning, you were the one responsible for putting it in its crate and loading it onto the ship. Only you didn't. You also knew the likes and dislikes of every member of Carmen's gang, and you used that knowledge so you could frame her."

Ben reached for Jersey's hat and pulled a long, squiggly nail from his hatband. "Just as I thought," he said. "No purple dot. Conclusive proof that you stole the third key. Do you admit it, or not?"

"What's the use?" Jersey said. "You kids are too sharp for me. Yes, I did it. And I'm not sorry. All I ever wanted was to be was an ACME agent, and Carmen destroyed my chances."

"No, you destroyed your own chances, Jersey," Maya said, "when you stopped playing fair." Then she pulled out a warrant and read him his rights. "Daley Bredd, alias Jersey Jones, you are under arrest for the theft of King Tut."

Epilogue
St. Petersburg, Russia

Alexander Nyetsky rushed over to meet Maya and Ben. "Helloing to you!" he called. "This exhibit is total my responsibleness. And thanks all to you, it is terrified success."

"Terrific success?" Maya guessed.

"Exactly mine words," Nyetsky said. He directed their attention to a silver medal on a ribbon around his neck. "See, I am no longer Deputy Director of Old, Dusty, and Interesting Things," he said proudly. "I am new Third Under-Secretary of Big and Wonderful New Things."

"Er—congratulations!" said Ben, edging away. "Listen, seeing as this is the opening day of the exhibition, I wonder if you could tell us where to find King Tut."

"Oh, sure enough," Nyetsky said. "First you are walking straight through hall with mirrors and then making left. You are not to miss it."

"Thanks a million," Ben said.

He and Maya walked through a room with dazzling chandeliers and paintings on the ceiling. Then they turned left as directed.

The chamber in which Tut lay was small and intimate. And the golden coffin sparkled with a sunlit radiance so bright that Maya and Ben almost had to shield their eyes.

Suddenly there was a flash of red at the far end of the room.

"Did I see a red trenchcoat?" Maya asked.

"You sure did," Ben replied.

"Carmen!" they both shouted, and ran after the fleeing figure.

Carmen dashed up the stairs and opened a window. Then she turned, smiled, and flipped a tiny card toward the two young friends. As it tumbled down, she jumped through the window and soared up into the air, lifted by an almost invisible cable toward a waiting hoversled.

"She's got a real hoversled!" Maya exclaimed.

"Incredible," Ben said, picking up the card.

It read:

DEAR BEN AND MAYA:

THANKS FOR HELPING TO CLEAR MY NAME. AND
FOR HELPING ME SEE HOW LOYAL MY PEOPLE REALLY
ARE. I KNOW WE'RE OPPONENTS, AND WE'RE SURE
TO MEET AGAIN. I ONLY WISH I COULD HAVE YOU ON
MY SIDE. THE CHIEF'S TRUST IN YOU IS WELL PLACED.
YOU'RE AS GOOD AS I EVER WAS.

146

DON'T MISS THE NEXT CARMEN SANDIEGO™ MYSTERY!

Highway Robbery

by Bonnie Bader & Tracey West
illustrated by S. M. Taggart

All Roads lead to . . . Carmen Sandiego?

Carmen Sandiego—the greatest thief in the world—has stolen Interstate 80, the longest and most traveled highway in the U.S. Motorists from coast to coast are stranded! Maya and Ben embark on a cross-country chase that takes them to some of the most radical roadside attractions either side of the Mason-Dixon line—everything from the 56-foot-high Big Chicken in Georgia to the Frog Fantasies Museum in Arkansas.

Can the Junior Gumshoes restore interstate travel before time runs out?